FOG

BRAD HARMER

SEVERED PRESS
HOBART TASMANIA

FOG OF WAR

WWW.SEVEREDPRESS.COM

ISBN: 978-1-925840-25-4

For my buddy Paul Selman
Purely because I know he'll get a kick out of having a book dedicated to him.
And that's as good a reason as any.

PROLOGUE

The mist crept through the dark village streets. No-one was home.

It seeped past locked shops, abandoned bicycles, and the carved, gently trickling fountain. Its ghostly fingers ran across railings, and its touch fogged display windows, as though pawing at the goods inside. All the buildings were dark, locked up for the night.

Perhaps for longer.

It rolled, gathering momentum and density, across the cobblestones of the village square, its ghost-like blue-grey probing and seeping across the village of Demetier.

It seemed to hesitate at the bloodstains, and at the empty shell casings that littered the ground in front of the small bakery; then it surged determinedly forward, obfuscating the macabre debris. It moved up and over the shattered glass of the storefront, covering the rolls and baguettes inside with a thin film of condensation, giving the food a loving touch, as if discovering a much loved toy from its childhood, now faded and covered with dust.

The mist spread further, filling the village square now, rising up to waist height in places. Frost seemed to spring up everywhere it touched, flowering and blooming in white crystals. Ghostly tendrils reached up the front doors of houses, wrapping around knockers and probing keyholes, trying to reach inside.

Only one building remained alive. Warm, amber light shone behind the shutters of *L'Agneau Abattu*. Voices and laughter sounded from inside and echoed across the empty village.

The mist crept down the street towards it.

More could be heard now than just the chatter of voices. There was also the clink of glasses, the rabble of drunken laughter, and occasional scraps of song creeping into the mix of merry-making.

The mist seemed spurred on, flowing down the short street to the inn, puffs of electric-blue-grey mist breaking off and rolling back onto itself as it travelled. If anyone had been there to see it, they would have found it strange, but there were only ten living souls in all of the village of Demetier, and they remained inside the safety and warmth of *L'Agneau Abattu*.

The mist reached the inn in seconds, and settled low to the ground, gently rolling despite the lack of any breeze. The sounds of drunken voices sang loudly - Marlene Dietrich's *Ich bin die Fesche Lola* - accompanied by raucous laughter and more glasses smashing.

The cobblestones beneath the mist were suddenly frosted, the ice crystals forming in a matter of seconds. They spidered up the brickwork of the inn, two feet high frosting melding the building with the floor.

Then the sounds came - slowly and quietly at first. The click of heels. The giggle of a child. Something dark and muttered.

The noises remained on the edge of hearing, and if anyone had been there to hear them, then they would have questioned whether they had truly heard them at all.

The door to the inn banged open sharply, and a young man in a German uniform stood silhouetted in the doorway, backlit by the glow from the fireplace. His jacket was unbuttoned, and his helmet sat crooked on his head. A mostly empty whiskey bottle hung in one hand.

"Will you shut that damn door?" roared a voice in German from inside the inn. "You're letting all of the goddamned heat out."

The young man stepped forward into the street, and called back inside. "You should see the weather out here. It's like nothing I've ever seen before. Have you ever seen anything like this before? I can't see more than ten metres."

"Shut the door!"

The young man turned back to face inside *L'Agneau Abattu.* "Doesn't it seem a little late in the year for you? I mean, I wouldn't expect this sort of fog past March."

SS-Obersturmführer Johann Seeliger - the squad commander - looked over from the bar and shouted again. "Private Schiller, I will not tell you again. Shut that damn door."

Schiller shrugged, re-entered the inn, and latched the door closed behind him. He sat back down at the table with his other squad mates, took a swing of his whiskey, and smiled at his friends' loud singing - which had now moved on to *Lili Marleen.* Dietrich was an unpopular figure at home - what with having renounced her German citizenship at the start of the war, and now selling War Bonds for the United States - but her works and her songs endured. Even Seeliger, the grumpy SS Officer in charge of the squad - didn't see fit to put a stop to their singing.

Schiller lit a cigarette, and closed his eyes.

The day had been tough. He was only twenty years old, and had already seen his share of what the war had to offer, but today had been hard.

Seeliger remained at the bar, drinking alone, refusing to mix with the rest of the squad. This didn't surprise Schiller. He'd yet to meet one of the SS who seemed even remotely human. They took their role as enforcers of the Nazi ideal deadly seriously.

A firm tapping sounded at the door that he had just closed.

Schiller's arm hairs rose, and he felt a cold sweat instantly appear on his forehead.

"Did you hear that?" he asked, leaping to his feet, the bottle falling to the floor and smashing.

"Hear what?" yelled one of his squad mates. Krehl, possibly, or maybe Vonhof.

"I...I heard someone knocking on the door," he mumbled. "Did no-one else hear that?"

Seeliger sneered from the bar. "Private Schiller, perhaps it's time for you to turn in for the night."

The door jolted hard on its hinges from two heavy, measured poundings.

The entire squad fell silent.

"Who the hell can that be?" whispered Krehl.

Seeliger stood, and pulled his Mauser from its holster, pointing it at the door. "Krehl, Vonhof...open the door. Let's see who our late-night caller is, and what they want."

Schiller and a couple of the others raised their MP40s to the doorway, ready to open fire as soon as the door was opened. Vonhof took one side of the doorway, with his pistol drawn. Krehl - a red-haired simpleton, who was nevertheless a crack shot with a rifle - held his pistol in his left hand, and reached toward the simple rope door latch with the other.

Schiller hadn't noticed the door latch before now. It seemed antiquated, like much in the small hamlet of Demetier. It felt as though the village had been untouched by the world for perhaps a hundred years. He supposed that this far out in the sticks, it took a while for news and even technology to travel. He felt a little sad, then, reflecting that it was a shame that war had finally come to this little corner of France.

Krehl lifted the loop of rope, and swept the door open smoothly.

There was nothing there but the fog.

It had grown in intensity in the few seconds that the door had been shut, and now the candlelight of the public house failed to illuminate much further than three or four feet into the town square. Its flickering yellow light simply made odd shapes and fleeting impressions of movement ripple across the grey smoke.

Seeliger shouted out from behind him. "Who's there? Show yourself in the name of the Führer!"

Krehl stepped out into the fog, raising his pistol, and sweeping left and right as he went. Again, it seemed as though strands of the fog moved and eddied around his arms and boots, as though the fog itself was trying to wrap around the young soldier and obscure him completely from sight.

Schiller heard Seeliger draw breath to yell something again, when they heard a sound in the distance. At first Schiller thought it must be a fox, or some other wild animal, but there was a melody in it that no animal could convey. It bent and flowed into a song that he half-recognised. A woman's voice, too faint and distant to judge how old she was, but he didn't imagine it was a child, nor a crone.

He let out a strangled grunt of shock and...fear?...as he realised what the voice was singing.

Lili Marleen.

There was a brief murmur as the realisation spread across the squad. Whoever it was out there had been listening, and was now singing the same song back to them. Schiller glanced quickly over his shoulder at the SS Officer. Seeliger's face was stoic, but there was no confidence in it, either. After a second, he nodded, as though confirming a decision to himself. "Move out. We must have missed one of them."

Schiller winced. The prospect of further repeating the task they had been working on all afternoon did not fill him with any enthusiasm. It had been almost more than he could bear.

Krehl - now about six feet from the doorway, and already becoming a dark figure in the fog - turned back to face them. “I don’t understand. There’s no light out here. I can’t see anyone. I can’t hear anyone except for the woman. I don’t know where she could be. She could be anywhere. There’s no point going looking for just one woman, surely?”

A shadowy blur burst from the dark fog, and collided with Krehl side on in a rugby tackle, catching him just under the ribs. The young man let out a strangled yelp, and was suddenly and completely obscured by the thick, grey clouds. The rest of the squad yelled his name and poured out of *L’Agneau Abattu*, shouting and sweeping their guns everywhere, trying to spot their friend and his mysterious assailant.

Schiller was the last to leave the pub and found himself lingering in the light from the doorway with Seeliger. A scream of terror and pain came from deep in the fog, across the village square, followed by a brief burst of machine gun fire, and then silence. The muzzle flash showed as a dull yellow pulse, no brighter than someone lighting a cigarette. Schiller stole another glance at the SS Officer, and wondered what he should do. It was obvious that they were under attack - most likely by resistance forces - but he couldn’t make out a damn thing through the fog.

SS Office Seeliger barked the names of his squad, desperately trying to call them back into order, when another yelp - this time sounding like Vonhof - sounded, much closer than the previous cry. Schiller swore under his breath and shivered as he saw dark figures moving and dashing through the fog. He impulsively fired off a burst of rounds from his MP40, and received a stern thwack on the back of the head from Seeliger.

“Cut that out, you moron! You’ll hit our own men! Only fire when you have a target.”

Another scream.

Schiller backed up to the doorway of the inn, its light seeming to cast barely any distance into the fog now, grey tendrils starting to seep over the threshold. “They’re being cut down like dogs. You really think the resista...”

Seeliger was nowhere to be seen.

Schiller felt his whole world drop away as he realised that he was alone in the fog of Demetier.

In the distance, the woman was still singing *Lili Marleen.*

He pulled his MP40 to his shoulder, and advanced away from the inn, into the fog. He figured that he stood more chance of finding his squad mates out in that grey darkness than he did loitering on the threshold.

Ten steps in and the glow from the door of *L’Agneau Abattu* was barely visible.

Then the figures around him began to appear.

They started out as simple, vague shapes in the fog, gradually coalescing into silhouettes. Some tall, some short; some men, some women and some children. Their faces and clothes remained obscured, but he could sense their shapes, and feel them moving slowly towards him.

His fight-or-flight adrenaline surged, and he fired wildly, the muzzle flash of his MP40 doing little to penetrate the vision-obscuring fog. He had no sense of where he was in the village, and what little light remained from the inn was now completely faded.

He knew he had to get out of the village of Demetier, but did not know which way to turn.

He cursed loudly as his shin collided with the stone fountain in the middle of the village square. The graze shocked him a little from his panic, and he tried to take stock of his surroundings. He knew that he must be nearer to the south of the square than the inn, as they had advanced into the town from that direction. That was right, wasn’t it? He couldn’t have gotten turned around already. Or could he?

He flinched and raised his gun once more. The sound of footsteps on the cobblestones echoed all around, dizzying and disorientating him. He called out the names of his missing friends, as well as the SS officer Seeliger, but there came no answer. Another series of footsteps came, from a different direction this time, or so it seemed. The reverberations made it difficult to be sure.

The wisps of grey fog trailed and curled over the lip of the stone fountain, skipping lightly over the surface of the water.

Again, he thought he saw shapes moving in the mist and called out to his colleagues, hoping, pleading that one of them would respond, or even just step out of the murk and greet him as a friend.

Then the voices came. Snatches of French conversation and odd words that he did not recognise at all. They hurtled around and through his ears, and he fell to his knees, sobbing. He knew then where the fog had come from, and why it was there. Through the tears in his eyes, he saw the figures in the darkness finally focus and step into his vision. There were none that he truly recognised, their faces still a little too shadowed for him to identify. The odd jacket, or scrap of dress material was recognisable, however, and he wished that it was not so.

He had just been following the orders he had been given. Surely they understood that? If he, or any of the others, had rebelled or resisted then they'd have felt the instant wrath of Seeliger's Mauser. They all had friends and family, wives and children, that they wanted to go back home to once the war was over. Surely they understood that it was them or him? They must surely have done the same thing, had they been in his position.

Shoulders slumping, he knew they would not understand, and truth be told, he did not truly understand it himself. It was a feeble excuse, and it would not save him.

Setting his machine gun on the cobblestones beside him, he buried his face in his hands, and softly prayed for forgiveness.

CHAPTER ONE

The journey from Dover had been a long and tiresome one, but Private Wilbert Alexander was grateful that it had at least been quiet. Although it had been a few months since the D-Day landings, there were plenty of signs of its passing. Landing craft lay deserted on the beach. German pillboxes and machine gun emplacements stood abandoned along the beach front, and at the sides of roads. The dead bodies had been cleared, of course, but the scars of the war were clearly marked in the soil. Tyre treads, tank traps, shell holes, barbed wire...the detritus of battle was everywhere.

The boat had been a rough ride across a choppy English Channel, but nothing had prepared him for the bone-jarring rattle of a four hour truck ride from the landing point to the village of Cherbourg. The jolting was bad enough, but on two instances a pot-hole (or shell hole, most likely) caused one of his fellow passengers' Sten guns to misfire with a loud retort, an avalanche of swear words, and a roar of laughter. Fortunately, it was the only gunfire they heard - there was not even the sound of distant shelling in the background - though the sky was often torn asunder by the roar of plane engines. Fighters and carrier planes were both patently in high demand.

It was not until they reached the base just outside of Cherbourg that Alexander felt that he'd actually arrived in a war zone. It started when a Churchill tank rolled past him, and the distinctive clank and whistle of the engine and treads gave him a Pavlovian thrill. All his drilling and training was complete. He was a tanker, in a war zone, fighting the Nazi hordes.

He'd joined the army as soon as he turned eighteen, and knew straight away that he had wanted to work with tanks. His father had been at the Battle of Cambrai, and his stories of the mechanised war machines had filled him with excitement and curiosity even at a very early age. To him, they sounded almost mythical.

Going to the cinema when he was a teenager, he'd felt a flush of adrenaline when he first saw newsreel footage of Monty's Desert Rats in Africa. He'd never admit it to anyone else, not even his closest friends and family, but he also loved seeing the Russian T-34s and even the German Panzers. He just loved tanks, totally and completely.

The truck rattled to a halt, and the passengers grabbed their bags and filed out. It was a short jump down from the back of the truck, and he had a mental image of tripping as he landed, breaking his ankle and completely eliminating himself from the war. He shook the image from his mind and followed the other new arrivals to the sorting office. He queued for what seemed like hours, but in actuality could not have been more than twenty minutes or so. There, his paperwork was quickly processed, and he was handed off to a tall, moustachioed officer to arrange his final placement.

He had expected the meeting to take place in an office of some kind, however ramshackle or makeshift it may have been. Instead, the Lieutenant simply grabbed his papers, and gestured for him to follow him outside. There, they sat down on some ammo boxes, and the officer took a closer look at his documents.

"Private Wilbert Alexander, from south London, aged eighteen."

It hadn't really been a question, but he still felt that it warranted an answer. "Yes, sir. Well, I turn nineteen next week, sir."

The Lieutenant nodded and scanned further along the paper with his pen, muttering to himself. "Trained at Bovington, as a loader/operator, yes?"

"Yes, sir. Learnt in a Churchill sir, as well as a little bit in a Valentine."

"Excellent. Is this your first time seeing combat?"

"Yes, sir. Other than in the films and on the newsreels, sir."

"Funnily enough, Alexander, we don't count those as being actual combat."

"No, sir."

The man looked up at him, and smiled, the moustache curling cartoonishly. "A little joke, Private. I knew what you meant. You're being assigned to Oliver Franklin's crew. They just lost their loader/operator, and they're desperate for a young and fit replacement."

"I'm sorry to hear that, sir."

"Oh, he's not dead. Bloody fool dropped a shell mid-loading procedure and broke his damned foot. He's going to be sat on the substitutes' bench for quite some time. It's no way for a soldier to get put out of the war, but I suppose that it beats a lot of the alternatives; certainly for his family. Barry, his name was."

"I'll endeavour to be more careful than that, sir."

The Lieutenant scribbled a few notes on his paperwork. "I'm glad to hear it. Franklin's crew operates a Comet. They're pretty new, but I can't imagine they're all that different from a Churchill once you're on the inside. Can't say I've had the stomach to work in one of those beastly things myself, but I've been damned glad to have them on my side on more than a few occasions. The Comet's got a hell of a gun on it, too. Nothing like the Tiger has, unfortunately, but I dare say it could take one out if it - that is, to say, if you - got lucky."

"I know a little of the Comet, sir, but I've never actually been inside one."

The Lieutenant stood, and tucked Alexander's papers under one arm. "Well, then. Follow me and I'll show you to your new home."

Alexander leapt to his feet, grabbed his bag, and jogged after the rapidly moving officer.

The base, though small, was hectic. There seemed to be a never-ending babble of noise, punctuated occasionally by the growl of a diesel engine. Soldiers and officers dashed here and there, all wrapped up in their own individual assignments that would eventually - one hoped - pull together into an Allied victory. Alexander reflected on just what a masterpiece of organisation the D-Day Landings had been. Three nations, across five beaches, as well as the paratrooper divisions. It was nothing short of a marvel.

He wondered if he should be attempting to make small talk with the Lieutenant, but the officer was marching along at a fair pace, and he was having to almost jog along as it was. It was obvious the man was in no mood for talking. Alexander supposed that he was just another checkbox on his "To Do" list; to be forgotten as soon as possible.

He felt a smile creep across his face when he reached the tanks. There must have been twenty, perhaps thirty, tanks - all standing ready with their crews either relaxing around them, or desperately finishing up some last minute engineering work. The clanks and curse words emanating from inside a Crocodile were testament to just how temperamental some types could be. He glanced at the tank, and suppressed a shiver. He was glad he didn't have to work inside one of those flame-thrower tanks. The prospect of having four hundred gallons of compressed nitrogen hanging off the back of your tank, while Tigers and Jagdpanthers fired at you, didn't seem like a good way to live your life to him. There were enough dangers in a war, and inside a tank, without literally adding fuel to the fire.

Several tanks down the line, he heard a thick Yorkshire accent cursing up a blue streak, accompanied by a loud, rhythmic banging. Sat atop the hull of a Comet was a large, red-faced man, already greying at the temples, whacking the seam between turret and hull with an oversized spanner. "You stupid, bastard, yellow, liver-eating, god forsaken, stupid, stubborn...gah!"

He threw the spanner down and his shoulders slumped with a large sigh.

"Is this Commander Franklin's tank?" asked the Lieutenant.

"What?" the Yorkshireman shouted over his shoulder, still not turning to face them.

The Lieutenant coughed. "I said, is this Commander Franklin's tank?"

The man still didn't turn around, and just yelled, "Franklin! Moustache is here for you!"

The Lieutenant's eye twitched, and Alexander suppressed a smirk.

After a moment, a man's head emerged from the main hatch, and threw them a smile. The man was probably in his early thirties, but long stubble and several layers of black grime made it difficult to say for sure. "Lieutenant Holcombe! To what do we owe the honour?"

The man - whom Alexander supposed must be Franklin, the tank commander - raised himself up out of the hatch with both arms to a seated position on the lip, and then smoothly stood up, walking casually across the hull to them. "What's this? A captured German spy?"

Lieutenant Holcombe smiled mirthlessly, and extended Alexander's paper's up to him. "This is Private Barry's replacement. Private Wilbert Alexander. He's fresh out of Bovington, but he seems pretty smart. Driven a few models it seems. I'm sure he'll get the hang of the Comet in no time."

Franklin didn't reach down to take the papers, leaving Holcombe holding them awkwardly. Instead he smiled down at Alexander. "Hello, Alexander. Think you can last to the end of the war without breaking your own foot?"

"Yes, sir."

"That's all I need, Holcombe. I can't be dealing with paperwork inside a tank. Is there anything else?"

Holcombe looked rattled, but accepting. "No, that's all. Alexander, good luck, and I'll leave you in Franklin's capable hands."

They saluted one another, and Holmcombe turned on his heel and strode off towards his next assignment.

Franklin watched him go and then hopped down, chuckling.

"I take it that you two don't get along, sir?"

"Franklin is fine. I don't go by 'sir' in a tank, or much outside of one for that matter. In there, I don't see that there's a hierarchy, you follow?"

"I..."

"Me, you - O'Brien, there - and the other two all have a job to do in that tank, and if one of us messes up then we're all dead, you see? I'm not better than any of you. If I drop the ball, you die. If you drop the ball, I die. Now, tell me, young man, does that sound like a chain of command to you?"

"I...don't..."

"No, it isn't. If it were a chain of command I'd be sat back in Paris, or even with Churchill in jolly old England, sipping port and worrying about supply lines and logistics and all other sorts of other super exciting things that I'm sure must fascinate all those lovely people, but I can't bear to give them the time of day. No. What we are is a team, you see. So, from now on, there'll be no addressing me as 'sir', you follow? It's Franklin, or Olly, if Franklin still strikes you as too formal. To be honest, if we run into Jerry, I'll just as likely answer to 'hey you'. Now, are we on the same page?"

Alexander forced a smile, still feeling a little awkward about it. "Yes, I think we are."

"Capital. Now, to answer your previous question: no, I like Holcombe just fine. He's a good egg, but he also possesses feathers that are simply just too much to resist ruffling. I enjoy making him squirm a little."

"Right. I see."

Franklin beamed at him. "I'm glad we've shucked the 'sirs' already. It took O'Brien here a month of Sundays to get them out of his system. Isn't that right, O'Brien?"

"Blow it out your arse," came the grumbled reply.

Alexander's eyebrows shot upwards, but Franklin just continued smiling. "He's our driver, and it has to be said that he's a dashed good one, too. Ah, yes, I suppose you'd best meet your counterpart."

Franklin balled up his fist and banged three times on the front hull of the tank. A single bang came in reply, and then another face popped up through the main hatch. A blonde man of twenty-five with a bandage running around his head levered himself out of the tank (although not as gracefully as Franklin had) and sauntered over to join them. "Hello, there. You Barry Number Two?"

Alexander laughed. "I suppose I must be. Alexander. Wilbert Alexander."

The young man squatted down and extended his hand. "Fred Cleveland. Gunner."

"You two will be working closely together, of course," put in Franklin. "Cleveland and I have been in the same crew since the start of the war. Natural born tanker, he is. You can trust him with anything. Ah, here comes the last of us now."

Turning, Alexander saw a young boy - perhaps even younger than he was - approaching with a large carton of cigarettes tucked under his arm, whistling some tune that was only partly audible above the rattle and clank of passing trucks, and the labours of

O'Brien hammering against the turret. "Hello!" The boy smiled in a thick Devonshire accent. "Who's this then? They sent us a replacement for old Barry already?"

Cleveland reached down and relieved the boy of the cigarettes, and laughed. "That's right. His name's Barry Number Two, but I'm sure it would be much nicer if you were to call him Alexander, what with that being his name and all."

Cleveland took the cigarettes away to the main hatch, and the young man stuck out his hand. "Steve Bright. Hull Gunner."

"Alexander, Loader/Operator."

Bright lit a cigarette and offered the pack to Franklin and Alexander, who both gratefully accepted. "It's French rubbish, of course, but the best I could scrounge up. Trust me, you'd hate to be stuck out there with a busted track, and nothing to smoke while you repair it."

"How soon are we heading out?"

Franklin exhaled a cloud of smoke. "Early tomorrow morning, or, at least as soon as O'Brien gets that turret repaired."

A stream of muttered curse words was the only response.

"What's the problem with it?" asked Alexander.

Bright cut in before Franklin could answer. "We haven't a clue. The turret's just making a devil of a noise whenever we try and turn it. Could be something up with the bearings, but whatever it is, we're sure O'Brien can fix it. Anyway, if we're off on the morrow, I've got stuff that I need sorting, if that's all right with you, Franklin. Could do with dashing off a letter to the wife."

"You only wrote to her yesterday," said the commander. "She won't have received that one, yet."

"I know, but I try and send her at least a few lines every day, sir."

Franklin smiled. "Yes, yes. Off you go. Be back here for five am, understand?"

Bright nodded and jogged off back in the direction of the barracks. Alexander felt two, three drops of rain strike him, and he suppressed a shiver. He didn't exactly want his first night here to be working on a faulty tank in the pouring rain. "If it's all right with you, sir - I mean, Franklin - I'd like to switch off for a little while, too. It's been a long journey, and I'd like to be fighting fit in the morning for you."

The tank commander waved him off. "Of course, of course. I was just about to suggest exactly that. You head off and get your head down. O'Brien, Cleveland and I can sort out this little problem."

CHAPTER TWO

Alexander felt as though his sleep had not been long enough, but supposed that in truth he could have slept the whole war away and not felt truly refreshed. The blankets had been thin and coarse and the mattress cold and hard, but the worst had been the non-stop background noises. The sound of the camp had been constant throughout the night: boots running, engines roaring and - now - the occasional rattle of machine gun fire, or the dull thud of artillery and bombs. Europe was in flames, and he was right in the thick of it.

He shivered into his boots, pulled on his uniform, gathered his equipment together, and jogged through the rain towards the Comet. The rain was so thin - but so constant - that it felt like running through a mist. His clothes felt soaked in a matter of moments, his boots sinking half an inch into the chewed up grass and mud of the base. He squinted his eyes against the rain and powered on.

"Steady on, lad," shouted a voice from his left. "Say, Alexander, steady on! You've gone straight past us!"

He spun around and jumped a little as he heard the engine of the Comet roar into life. "Come on, man! We don't want to have to leave without you!"

He jogged the remaining distance over to the tank, clambered up on top, aided by the extended hand of Franklin, and was gently shoved in the direction of the main hatch atop the turret. "What's our mission?" he shouted as he backed toward the open hatchway.

"We'll know when we get there!" the commander shouted behind him.

Inside the tank was the rattle and roar of the engine, echoing and reverberating off of every surface. He squeezed himself down and around the others, gently tapping them a friendly 'hello' on the shoulder as he did so, finally seating himself in the position filled by the loader/operator. Fred Cleveland smiled at him in a friendly way. "Welcome aboard!" he shouted, though Alexander picked up more from reading his lips than he did from actually hearing him. He returned his thanks, and held on tight as the tank roared up and into life.

He always loved this feeling. When the engine revved, and the tracks began to bite into the soil, propelling the "landship" forward, it felt nothing less than glorious. The bangs and rattles of small rocks kicked against the hull, the instant and pungent smell of diesel fumes in the air, and the hissing rattle-wheeze of the bogeys made him smile. He looked up and around at the rest of the crew (although Franklin was still top-half out of the turret, leaving only his legs visible), and if they weren't outright smiling, then he could at least see the same glee and satisfaction in their eyes.

"No feeling like it, right?" shouted Cleveland.

Alexander was about to shout back a reply when Bright cut in from his hullgunner position, squinting through a gun sight. "No, sir, you're damned right about that!"

Alexander held on tight, and felt the tank thrown back and forth a little by the stop-start speed changes necessary to navigate their way out of the base and into the war zone. It seemed they were kept waiting for an interminably long time at one junction, the temperature in the tank creeping up steadily, the sweat starting to soak into his shirt and underwear, mixing with the cold rain water to make him feel even damper than he already felt.

Finally, the engine roared once more and they pulled off and into the French countryside.

Alexander was excited to be a part of the tank crew, but his sleep deprivation, combined with the white noise of the engine, the warmth and the rocking motion was actually in danger of sending him off to sleep. He bit on his tongue to wake himself up, the pain and adrenaline snapping his eyes back open sharply, and tried to listen out for some vague hint as to where the tank might be headed, but he couldn't garner a single clue.

Eventually, after what seemed like hours - but his watch assured him was a little under forty minutes - Franklin gave the order for the tank to stop, and he heard the engine rev down and eventually stop with a sigh and a whistle.

"Coming up top for a break, old chap?" Cleveland asked, tapping him on the knee. "Always time for a smoke break."

"Uh...of course."

Alexander was the last to leave the tank, levering himself awkwardly out of the turret hatch. The sun was just rising over the horizon, casting everything into an orange and dark blue light. Blinking around, he saw that the tank had stopped at the side of the road, near a small copse of trees. The road - mostly gravel and mud, churned up by the tracks and wheels of the combined British, American and Canadian forces - led off ahead, and he could make out a small town or large village a couple of miles in the distance. A supply plane roared overhead, causing him to involuntarily duck. He'd been a kid during the early days of The Blitz, and aeroplanes still rattled him on some primal level.

Franklin lit up a cigarette and struggled with unfolding an oversized map. "Right, chaps. Here's what we're up to today. We're to proceed in an easterly...oh, dash it all!"

A gust of wind had caught the map, causing it to buckle and ripple in the commander's hands. Chuckling, Cleveland stood up and assisted him, holding it up and out so that the assembled crew could see what he was pointing at.

Franklin mumbled his thanks, and then gestured across the map with a sweeping motion. "Right, lads, as you can see here, this is France, which is the fair country that we are currently very privileged to occupy. The German forces are steadily being pushed back - which is, of course, rather an over simplification of the facts, but it's the general gist of things, all right. Our job, fortunately, is a relatively simple one."

"Sir?" Alexander raised his hand.

"What is it, Alexander? And, please, dispense with the formalities. I don't want to have to tell you again."

Alexander blushed, glancing nervously at his own hand. "I…are we operating alone, out here? I had assumed that we'd be part of a...uh...larger fighting group."

"Sometimes we are, Alexander. And sometimes there are missions like this where one tank operates out on its own. At the moment, we are on a simple patrol. We follow the little route that Holcombe was kind enough to draw on the map for us, take note of anything we deem to be of strategical importance, engage any enemy where feasible, and provide assistance to any of the indigenous population where we can."

"An everything and nothing job," Cleveland muttered around a cigarette.

"That about covers it," agreed Franklin. "Any questions?"

"How long we supposed to be out here for?" Bright asked, one arm hung lazily across the hull machine gun.

"A couple of days. There are some refuelling points that Holcombe very kindly marked on his little map for us. Isn't that sweet of him?"

"Great. Sleeping atop the tank. My favourite."

The sun was climbing towards midday as they followed the road down into the small village. Alexander was riding up top, trying to make himself as comfortable as possible on the tank's hull, with Franklin's upper body sticking out of the turret hatch next to him. The weather seemed very changeable that day. Sometimes - when the sun crept out from behind cloud cover - it felt comfortingly warm, so much so that he could have happily dozed off if he wasn't concerned about falling off of the tank. At other times, the wind whipped up sharply, and he had to resist the urge to pull the collar of his jacket up around him as a shield against its cruel bite.

As they made their way down the road towards the village, it slowly began to dawn on him that it was not as idyllic as it had first appeared. What was likely once a dirt, country road had been churned up to a cloying, muddy paste by the passing of numberless boots, wheels and tracks. The sides of the road were marked with lengths of razor wire - far too extreme a solution for keeping animals in their paddocks; their purpose was obviously military.

He gazed across a field, one arm leaning against the turret and thought he could see two or three trees with parachute canopies - or at least the remains of them - stretched across their branches. Several of the fields were marked with craters, the earth within them blackened by the heat of the artillery round that had created them.

"You know," said Franklin, "when this is all over - and I think that'll be soon - I'd like to come back to France. I want to see what it's like when it hasn't been walked all over by the Nazis for five years. I want to see vineyards, and the children playing. Maybe go to Paris, and see The Louvre. Take the missus for a week or two."

"Yes," agreed Alexander. "I know what you mean. It...it feels sad, here. This isn't what it should look like."

"Imagine how the locals feel. Can you imagine this kind of destruction, this kind of depression hanging over the British countryside? The Yorkshire Dales littered with tank traps? The Kent countryside bombed into burnt earth? It makes me furious just to think of it. No wonder the Resistance is so active. They want their country back."

Alexander nodded. “Yes. Turns your stomach, doesn’t it?”

The tank changed gear with a lurch, and one track slowed down as they turned around a corner. As they came around the bed, Alexander and Franklin got a better view of the village ahead of them, and it only served to confirm the feelings they already had.

What had once been a nice, cobbled town square was pasted with mud and dirt. Several sections of the road were cracked and buckled, either from heavy arms fire, or the passage of large vehicles. Children still ran and played in it, dirty faces and gap-toothed smiles flashing by as they chased after a ball or hoop. Parents darted from out of doorways, breaking off conversations to shepherd their children out of the way of the tank.

Franklin’s eyes followed a young, brown-haired girl clutching a rag doll, jogging to her mother’s arms, covering her ears against the rattling wheeze of the Comet’s engine. It made him think of his own daughter, Rosemary, who was around her age, back home in London. He hoped to see her again, and soon. Attempting to distract himself from his own reverie, he leaned sideways and spoke quietly to Alexander, just loud enough to be heard over the tank’s engine. “You notice anything unusual, here?”

Alexander looked around. “The people. They...they don’t want us here, but they know there’s nothing they can do. You can see it in their eyes. It’s like...acceptance, but with a touch of resentment.”

“There’s that,” agreed the tank commander, “but I was referring to something a little more tangible, if you follow me. Look up.”

Alexander looked up at the buildings around them. “There’s no windows. Well, there are windows, but there’s no glass in them.”

"Artillery," nodded Franklin. "The sound wave...as I understand it, at least...the shockwave, or the noise, from an incoming shell can be enough to shatter the glass."

"That must be terrifying."

"You're not from London, are you?"

"Canterbury."

"Ah, I'm from Dover, myself. Well, originally, anyway. Now living in Knightsbridge, London. Anyway, it was like that during the Blitz. I mean, it never happened to us, thankfully, but you'd be forever walking down streets where there was nothing but remnants of shattered glass in the window."

Alexander suppressed a shiver, and was glad that he lived in a place that had more or less escaped the terrifying Blitz.

The tank turned at the centre of the town square, swinging right to a two o'clock heading. The engine roared monstrously as only one track pulled the weight along on its axis. Alexander saw some of the village children tuck under their parent's arms in fright, and he realised that they must have been living in mortal fear for months, now. He wished there was something that he could do to convince them there was nothing to fear from them, but he knew that there was not. He was just another foreign soldier, tearing up their village, and smashing through their lives.

Franklin obviously picked up on his mood, and clapped him comfortingly on the shoulder. "I know, old bean, I know. There's nothing that we can do besides hope that this is all over quickly, and that lives across the world can heal as quickly and as best as they can."

The tank pushed on through the village, and in a matter of moments, they were on the outskirts.

Alexander had hoped that he'd pushed through and seen the worst of it by now, but there was no such luck.

His eyes fell upon the destroyed building, and he felt anger and sadness well up inside of him. The house was a simple, small dwelling, but it had been someone's home, once, and now the blackened charred remains stood there like a rotten tooth.

"Artillery round, gone off course," whispered Franklin. "Rotten luck. Positively rotten."

It was the touches of humanity that made it worse. If it had been just a shell of fire-blackened brick and mortar, then he could have written it off as just a ruined building. It was the pictures still hanging on the wall, canvas long gone, the frames gaping emptily and the sad, lonesome shape of a rocking chair that prevented him from doing so. A cenotaph of memories.

There was no sign of what had happened to the family that once lived there, and Alexander could only hope for the best. Hope that they had escaped the carnage and the rotten luck, and that they were somewhere - near or far - rebuilding their lives.

In another moment, the tank was back in the countryside, leaving the town behind them a mere memory. Another ash thrown out by the fire that consumed the world.

CHAPTER THREE

They stopped briefly for lunch, and to let the engine rest for a while. Alexander found himself chatting with O'Brien while Franklin and Cleveland went over the map again, plotting out their journey for the next few hours. O'Brien was a lot more approachable than he had been when Alexander first encountered him working on the tank. He was obviously still cantankerous, but he was at least open to a conversation with his new crew member. "The commander was saying that this is your first mission out here?" he asked in a thick Yorkshire accent.

"Yes, that's right. They sent me here straight from Bovington, more or less."

O'Brien finished the last of his stodgy and tasteless combat rations and lit a cigarette. "I remember my first deployment. Africa. Driving a Cromwell around the desert. I expected to be thrown straight into adventure and glory as soon as we arrived. We were there nine months and I think I saw a grand total of three German units. All scouts on motorbikes. Didn't fire a single shot."

"Have you seen much action since then?"

O'Brien hadn't heard him. "That was when I learned that war was going to be mostly being bored off my arse and occasionally getting the news that someone I'd sat in the mess with was dead. Not much has changed since then."

"You sound almost as if you regret it."

O'Brien shook his head. "I've seen enough. Felt bullets strike the metal next to my head a few too many times for comfort. Never taken a hit from a Jerry tank, thank the heavens. The giants they've got now, they'd have torn us all to shreds. The Comet here may stand more of a chance, but most of our tanks don't stand a chance against a Tiger."

"I've still yet to see anything. Feels like the Germans are a long way from here."

O'Brien flicked the ash from his cigarette and studied the glowing tip. "No regrets. I'd rather have a quiet war than a dangerous one."

"Of course."

"The Germans might be a long way from here, but we can't assume that much, you know. That's what gets you killed in a war: assuming that the enemy doesn't care that you're there. If you're cautious, and keep your head down just as much as you can, then I think you'll come out of this all right."

Alexander nodded, and lit a cigarette of his own. He straightened up and looked around half-expecting to see a German soldier peering at him from the trees, or perhaps hear the scream of a German fighter tearing across the sky.

Franklin made his way over to them, still smiling his constant, reassuring smile. "All right, chaps. We think we've got a handle on where we're going."

"Perhaps you'd like to let me know where that is?" asked O'Brien. "I'm the one steering the bloody thing."

"Well, it's an easy job for you, at least. We're sticking to this road for another hour or two yet. There's a bridge a few miles down that you'll need to go slow and easy over, but after that, it's relatively plain sailing."

"Well, that's something," muttered O'Brien, flinging his cigarette butt to the ground and grinding it into the mud with his boot heel. "Nice to be able to just drive in a straight line for a change.

Maybe I'll even be able to have a quick snooze while we're trundling along."

Alexander didn't have the luxury of travelling up on the top of the tank this time. Franklin stood half-in and half-out of the hatch in the main turret, shouting commands down to Alexander when necessary, which it was then his job to relay to O'Brien, sat at the master steering controls for the thirty-two ton tank. He felt that thrill of excitement again - the sheer joy of knowing that he was living his boyhood dream of actually working alongside (and inside) the war machines that had filled his head since he was young. Across the hot, dark interior, he made eye contact with Bright, the young hull gunner, and saw his own enthusiasm and happiness reflected in them.

"Best job in the world, isn't it" he yelled, his thick Devonshire accent somehow making him more understandable in the rattling, roaring, wheezing cacophony inside the Comet.

Alexander smiled back to him. "Wouldn't swap it for all the tea in China!"

Franklin yelled down some more instructions. "Bridge coming up now, just over the crest of the next little hill, here."

Alexander held up a hand to show that he'd heard, then hobbled over to O'Brien - the cramped confines of the tank making a hobble all that was possible - and yelled, "The bridge is coming up. Just over the next hill. Franklin can see it, but you probably can't from down here."

"Right you are..." muttered O'Brien, an unlit cigarette hanging from his mouth. "What exactly am I supposed to do with this information?"

"I guess you...uh...what do you normally do?"

"Fuck's sake, lad. Ask him."

"Uh...right. Right you are, skip."

Alexander hobbled back over to the turret entrance. He'd hit his calves and hands on sharp metal edges so many times now that he didn't really feel the pain anymore. They just ached constantly from a hundred bangs, bruises, scratches and scrapes. "Uh, commander?"

"What is it, loader/operator?" Franklin asked sarcastically, and Alexander remembered that he hated being addressed formally.

"What should O'Brien do about the upcoming bridge?"

"Tell him to drop speed, we're only about two or three hundred yards away. Drop down steadily, and be ready to come to a complete stop if we need to."

"Right you are."

*Bang, scuffle, scrape, biff, scratch...*and he was back behind O'Brien. He leaned forward into his ear. "Slow ahead. Boss man says that the bridge is just a couple of hundred yards in front of us. We may need to go dead slow across it."

O'Brien coughed, and muttered sarcastically under his breath. "'Slow ahead'. Yeah, I can go slow ahead. Come down here and-"

Alexander felt the impact before he heard the noise and instantly thought that they were done for. He was hurled sideways, slamming his shoulder and helmet hard against the inside wall of the tank. He saw O'Brien and Bright rock in their seats but manage to stay upright, gripping hold of what little padding there was, or bracing themselves against the frame of the tank. There was a whirring clatter as Franklin dropped down the turret into the body, sealing the hatch above him, fully "buttoning down" the tank.

"What the hell was that?" O'Brien yelled back over his shoulder. "Did you see it? Is it Jerry?"

Alexander gasped as he saw Franklin. The commanding officer was spattered with road dust, and had a terrible gash running across his forehead, streaming blood down into his eyes. "I didn't see anything," he yelled, trying to blink his eyes clear. "Something hit us, but I don't know where from. I didn't hear or see anything. Is anything damaged down here?"

Cleveland could just be heard over the engine. "Doesn't look like the hull's damaged. We took a bloody hard knock to the right, so they must be to our left."

"Main gun loaded," shouted Alexander, making the final preparations.

Cleveland began turning the turret of the tank to the left, trying to get a view of what had assaulted them. "I don't see anything," he called down, surprisingly calm. "O'Brien, how's mobility?"

Alexander was hurriedly trying to clean and dress the wound on Franklin's forehead, and relayed the message breathlessly over his shoulder. "O'Brien? Mobility?"

O'Brien threw some levers and the tracks kicked into life. Alexander could feel them moving, but knew something was wrong.

"Left track is fucked!" O'Brien yelled. "We're sitting ducks!"

"Kill the engine!" Cleveland shouted. "No use burning the fuel. I'll see what I can see from up here."

For a moment the only sounds were the humming and grinding of the turret moving up above them, the tiny sounds of Alexander ripping bandages for the commander's head wound, and the muttered curses coming from the cantankerous driver.

"There's nothing there," called down Cleveland. "Permission to go up top and take a look?"

"Be careful," replied Franklin, raising one hand to the bandage to maintain the pressure. "And take Alexander up with you."

Alexander nodded his assent and left him in as comfortable a position as could be maintained, and clambered toward the main hatch. Cleveland was waiting for him to arrive. "Ready? Sidearm?"

Alexander drew his pistol, wondering what good it would do them if they were to run into a Tiger. "Sure."

Cleveland threw open the hatch and climbed up, training his pistol ahead of him, eyes darting around for any sign of movement.

The daylight felt blinding after more than an hour in the dark cacophony of the Comet, and Alexander had to blink several times. He wondered that if there had been a Tiger sat there directly in front of him, whether or not he would even have registered its presence.

"Fucking hell," Cleveland muttered ahead of him. "Well, the good news is that I don't think we're in much danger. The bad news is that O'Brien is going to be bloody furious."

Alexander's eyes adjusted to the bright sunlight and he saw what had happened. Jumping down from the top of the tank to the ground, he assessed the damage.

The front of the left hand track of the tank was hovering just above a small ditch, blacked by the explosion they had felt inside. The track was split at one of the joins, several segments missing, the two ends of the remaining track splayed up and open as if beseeching the heavens.

"Panzerfaust?" Alexander asked nervously, spinning around to keep his eyes open for any nearby Nazi troops.

"No, if they thought the Panzerfaust had crippled us, we'd be overrun by now, or one of their own tanks would have turned up to finish the job. Look. Most of the damage is to the ground. We were just unlucky that it broke the track."

"What did?"

"Land mine. Anti-personnel one, by the look of it. Would have made a real mess of our infantry, so all things considered I'm really glad we took the brunt of this one."

"O'Brien's going to be pissed off about the track," muttered Alexander. "Looks a relatively clean break, though, so I think that we could be back on the road inside of an hour."

Cleveland banged three times on the side of the tank, the crew's informal signal that it was all clear and that they could come outside. "That doesn't mean that O'Brien won't complain. The man loves a good old grumble."

"Jerry must have left this as they fell back; hoping to do some spiteful damage, or at least slow us down. It's as you say: it's a good thing a tank ran into this rather than someone's boot."

"Could be the Germans, though to be honest it's probably just as likely to have been the Resistance. They're good lads, but a trifle uncaring. Rather a Cavalier attitude to a lot of things. They could have left this to catch a German unit and it might never even have crossed their minds that an Allied force could run into it. Or a lonely shepherd. That would have made a bally old mess, eh?"

Franklin, O'Brien and Bright clambered out of the tank and - as expected - O'Brien rolled his eyes dramatically.

"Oh, for fuck's sake. Land mine? A fucking land mine took us out of the running? We're supposed to be able to just steamroller over these things. Isn't that the whole reason they started deploying tanks in the first place?" His shoulders slumped and he let out a resigned grunt. "Never mind. I'll get the tools and get on it."

"It's a clean break," Cleveland called after him as he headed to the rear of the tank. "We should be back on the road inside an hour."

"Aye, we will with you helping me, Cleveland, son. Sounds to me like you just volunteered to get your hands dirty."

Franklin chuckled and clapped Cleveland hard on the shoulder, rocking him a little on his feet. "I say, that was awfully kind of you to volunteer, Cleveland, old boy."

Cleveland returned a wry smile, and lit a cigarette. "Well, make sure the rest of you don't overdo it. Keep watch for Jerry; or well meaning Resistance."

The two of them set to work repairing the track. It wasn't especially hard work, but it was fiddly at times, and every frustration they encountered was made audible by the grumbling basso of O'Brien.

Alexander, Franklin and Bright took it in turns keeping watch. One stood atop the tank, looking in all directions, while the other two squatted at the side of the road, smoking and chatting. They took ten minute shifts, and Alexander had just finished his second when a cheer from the front of the Comet indicated that the work had been completed.

"Okay, we're back on the road," yelled O'Brien.

"Sterling stuff, chaps," smiled Franklin. "Okay, everyone, I'd like to make up for lost time, but to be honest, I don't know how practical that'll be with that bridge coming up. What's more, we've now got to allow for running into more landings, wire, or all other sorts of nasty traps. O'Brien, take it slow and steady, but let's see if we can put the pedal down a little when we're back in the open country again."

"Right you are," O'Brien muttered, throwing his cigarette butt to the ground and clambering up the side of the tank. "All right, chaps, you heard the man, let's get this show on the road."

Alexander felt the closeness and darkness of the interior of the Comet much more now that he'd had a refreshing break on the outside. It was strange. He found that he was instantly missing the feel of the breeze on his skin. The tank felt ten times hotter than when he had exited it with Cleveland just an hour ago. He was painfully and fully aware of the drops of sweat running down his back and ribs, and couldn't get away from the idea of letting the French breeze blow them from his naked body...but here he was. Crushed up in a tin can with nothing to savour except the odd comfort of the white noise of the engine, and the smell of Bright's farts, and the constant tobacco stink of O'Brien.

He couldn't see where they were going, he could only hear odd snatches of conversation between Cleveland and Franklin, and occasionally Bright would turn and smile at him in the hot, humid darkness.

It felt as though he'd almost nodded off a couple of times, and he was grateful that no-one seemed to have noticed. He still hadn't quite recovered from his journey from England, and the heat and the rocking motion was almost too much for him.

CHAPTER FOUR

The rest of the day passed without incident, and when they finally did stop for the day, Alexander fell out like a light. He didn't dream, which was unusual for him, as he usually had particularly vivid ones, which he could recall in extreme detail upon waking. This time, however, it was as though no time had passed at all. He had closed his eyes, and then - in a flash - Bright was gently shaking his shoulder, bringing him around. "Brekkie time, old chap. More of the British army's finest rations. Spared no expense. If you concentrate really hard, then you can pretend that it's bacon and eggs at The Savoy, served to you by the prettiest waitress you ever saw. The coffee isn't too bad, either. You can't even taste the acorns."

Alexander rubbed sleep from his eyes and gratefully accepted a mug of the ersatz coffee. "No activity during the night, I take it?"

"We'd have woken you if there had been. We all took a shift at keeping watch, but you've the commander to thank for your lie in. He said you'd had a harder day than the rest of us had, what with your long journey and all that."

Alexander felt a little guilty. "Oh. You needn't have done that on my account."

Bright shrugged and sat on the ground next to him, leaning back against the front of the tank. "That's quite all right. Your first day on the job is always a killer, isn't it?"

"You've got the right of that."

"So, what's your story? Franklin said you're a Bovington chap?"

"That's right. Well, I'm from Dover, but I did my training over there."

Bright rolled a cigarette and smiled. "Is that right? I was in Bovington, too. Must've only missed you by a few months. I mean, you must be the same age as me."

"I'm eighteen."

"Ah, I'm nineteen, so near enough. So, what's your story? Just fancied firing a bloody big gun for a living?"

Alexander chuckled. "Well, yes, I suppose I did. I just loved seeing the tanks in the old newsreels, you know? I saw them roaring along and I thought to myself 'Dash it, that's what I want to do.'."

Bright reached behind him and slapped a hand to the tank's hull, affectionately. "I think it's the same story for all of us, but what about the rest of it? You got yourself a girl at home?"

Alexander took a swig of coffee to hide his embarrassment. That was one aspect of life in which he was woefully inexperienced. "No, not exactly. A couple who I think would say yes, if I asked, but I...I guess I wanted to get this business out of the way first. I'm still living with my mother and father. My father's a journalist for *The Times*."

"I say, that's pretty prestigious, isn't it? Not just the local rag, eh?"

"Yes, we're all very proud of him. What about yourself? Oh, yes, you have a wife at home, don't you? You were writing her letters when we were back at the base."

Bright lit his cigarette, and once again playfully slapped the tank. "Aye. Maisie. Margaret, but she prefers Maisie. Lovely little thing, and a simply beautiful cook."

"How did you meet? You seem young to be married already."

"I suppose we are, a little, but it just seemed the right thing to do. We lived on the same street, that's all. Used to play and run riot together all the time. She was just one of those people, you know; one of those faces that seem to crop up again and again. We just hit it off, I suppose and one thing led to another."

"Any little ones?"

"Gosh, no, not yet. Like you, I want to get all of this business out of the way first. Maisie is a worrier, though. That's why I send her letters every day - or as often as I can get to a mailing point. It's part because I think she'd be interested in what's happening, but also just to kind of remind her that I'm still alive."

"You don't think she'd forget, surely?"

Bright shrugged. "You hear stories of the things wives get up to while their husbands are away. I'd hate that to happen to me."

"You're a rotten shit, Bright, you know that?" came the thick Yorkshire accent of O'Brien. Looking up, they saw the older man standing on the tank above them.

Bright got to his feet. "What do you mean by that, Nicholas? Talking like that back home would get you a thick ear."

O'Brien smiled to himself, and wiped his hands on a dirt and lubricant soaked rag. "Oh, aye? Well going into every knocking shop in Paris would get you a thick ear from your lovely Maisie back home, don't you think? You were sure to mention all those lovely girls in your letters back home to her, right? I'd hate to have to write to her myself and fill in all the details you left out."

Bright sneered and kicked at a clod of earth. "I don't know what you're talking about, old man."

"I think you do, but that's your business. Well, yours and Maisie's, that is. Maybe she's fine with you philandering with every whore in France, but, well..."

Bright pouted and shrugged. "I don't know where you're getting your ideas from, old man. You've been getting too many fumes off of that engine, I should say."

He kicked at another sod, and shuffled off to see what the others were up to.

"Sanctimonious little prick," muttered O'Brien, before looking down to Alexander. "Lots of soldiers play away from home, you know, but it's the double standard I don't like with him. That and...well...you saw the bald faced lie, there, right? I don't know who he thinks he's fooling, but it's not me; nor any of the rest of the crew for that matter."

Alexander lit a cigarette. "Why does he lie?"

O'Brien shrugged. "Who knows? Maybe he doesn't even like admitting it to himself. It could be that he's feeling guilty about sowing his wild oats now that he's already married. Could be that he, well, could be that he's honestly worried about upsetting her. Tell you what I reckon though, son. I reckon it's because if he admits that he's been doing it, it opens up the possibility that little Maisie's been at it as well. He doesn't like having to picture her with the next door neighbour, the butcher's boy, his brother...you can imagine the rest."

"There's a certain sense to that, I suppose," agreed Alexander. "A sad situation, really, isn't it?"

O'Brien made a non-committal grunt. "I hope it comes to nothing, that's for damn sure."

A strange, garbled, metallic noise interrupted their conversation. It took him a moment to figure out what it was, by which time O'Brien had already bellowed across to the tank commander. "Franklin! Radio!"

The commander swung himself up to the turret, dropping down with a metallic 'thunk' sound.

O'Brien tipped the remains of his coffee mug onto the ground. "That's got to be bad fucking news."

"How do you mean?" Alexander asked.

"I mean that if everything was going fine, and that there were no changes to the plans, and we could just continue on with our little journey, and get back to base sooner rather than later, then we wouldn't be hearing a peep from command. That they're radioing us out in the field is a bad sign. It means something has changed. It means that there's work to be done."

"That's not always a bad thing, surely? It could mean the Germans have surrendered. It could mean anything."

O'Brien shook his head. "The Germans will take the fight to Berlin before they surrender, you can trust me on that. They're bloody fanatics."

Alexander stood up, wiping his trousers clean. "Do you think it's true what they say? About the camps I mean?"

Cleveland had overheard them, and joined in the conversation. "Oh, come now. I'm sure things are a bit tough over there. I mean, I certainly wouldn't like to be occupied by the Jerries, but you don't believe that rot about death camps, surely?"

"I don't know," muttered Alexander. "It just sounds...odd, don't you think?"

"Oh, please. You really think that the Nazis could orchestrate the arrest, incarceration and extermination of 'thousands' of people without it being noticed? You know the bloody Germans. They'd never stop bragging about it if they could," he raised a hand as O'Brien went to say something. "Now, I'm not saying they don't have labour camps, or POW camps, or somewhere to keep the communists and the traitors and - yes - maybe some Jews, but some of the things you hear...no. Just not possible."

O'Brien didn't look convinced. "If the Germans are one thing, it's organised. If anyone could do it, they could."

Cleveland waved it away. "Well, possibly. I don't see how they could maintain a project the size of what you say and manage to fight a war on two fronts as well. That just doesn't make a lick of sense."

Alexander had been about to point out that a world war was exactly the sort of smoke screen that would make it possible for the death camps to exist, but he was stopped by Franklin re-emerging from inside the Comet. "Okay, chaps. Gather round. New orders from HQ."

Bright, still sulking a little, joined the rest of them at the side of the tank. "What is it, skip?"

"Some Yankee Doodles have run into a spot of bother about an hour from here. They were passing through a little village; Demetier, I think Holcombe said it was called. At least, I think it was Holcombe. Those stiff upper lip chaps all sound the same over the wireless, don't they? Anyway, that's not important. The story is that the Yanks have run into a spot of bother in that village - run into Jerry, we assume - and have requested some assistance. As luck would have it, we're only about an hour's trundle away from them, so that's what we're up to today."

"Bloody Yanks," muttered Cleveland. "Their heads are too bloody big by half, if you ask me. They seem to think that they'll win this bloody war single handed. It's all a big, bloody Hollywood movie to them, isn't it?"

"Well, they had the humility to ask for help this time."

"Aye, when they're being shot at and need a tank to hide behind."

"Be that as it may, we've volunteered to help so, get to your places. We're on our way."

Alexander went to raise his hand to ask a question, and managed to stop himself halfway. You're not a bloody schoolboy any more, he chastised himself. "Do we have any idea what opposition we're going to run into?"

Franklin grimaced. "Not a bally clue, I'm afraid. I'd be surprised if it's all that much, though. What German forces there are around here are pretty much routed, so they'll be panicked and under supplied, whoever they are. I certainly don't think we're going to run into a battalion of Tigers in a little farming village."

"It wouldn't need to be," muttered O'Brien, hurrying to finish his cigarette, so he could climb back into the tank. "It's only got to be two or three Nazis setting up a bunch of landmines along the road to the village. You all remember what happened earlier, right?"

Alexander did, and the idea of more than one of those going off underneath him or - even worse - being struck with one of the German Panzerfausts filled him with cold fear.

"That's enough nattering for now, ladies," Franklin chivvied them along. "Let's get this show on the road, as they say. Those Yanks need our help."

There was a muttered round of affirmations and grunts of acceptance, and the crew began climbing back into the tank.

To Alexander, something felt different this time. All day yesterday he'd been filled with nothing but pure exhilaration, feeling the thrill of riding a six hundred horsepower, thirty-two ton war machine into battle. It felt like something from straight out of the American comic books that sometimes showed up at the newsagent, full of the adventures of The Human Torch, Namor and Captain America smashing up the Japanese and German forces. He supposed he'd actually been a little too old for them, but he'd positively devoured them, nonetheless. He wished that he'd had a little brother he could have left them to, but he was an only child. The comics sat under his mattress in his bedroom back home. Maybe he'd be able to pass them onto his own son - or daughter - one day.

Today, though, something felt different.

He supposed that part of it could have been due to the incident with the land mine. It was the first time he'd been, if not 'under fire' exactly, then at least the target of an enemy attack. It hadn't been a nice feeling at all. It had hit home that this was no longer a training mission. This was a very real danger to his life, and all bets were off.

It had been before that, though.

It had been that bombed out house back in the village they had passed through.

He kept seeing it in his mind's eye, a towering monument to the harsh, uncaring realities of the war.

It was one thing for a military man to be fired at. He had signed up for the job, he'd been trained, and he was driving around behind four-inch thick armour.

The occupants of that house had been none of those things. They hadn't volunteered to be a part of anything, and they certainly hadn't received any preparation or protection. They probably hadn't even thought that the war would ever come to their tiny little village, full of humble lives and gentle pastimes. It had been nothing short of cruel fate that had struck their home, and they deserved better.

There was not even an attempt at conversation inside the tank this time. This was no longer a simple patrol into the French countryside - nothing much more than a jolly day out, or so it had seemed when they had first opened up the engine. Now, they were engaged on a mission, tasked with saving lives.

And, if it came down to it, ending them.

The radio chattered gently behind him, and Franklin answered it. Alexander couldn't hear the words that were spoken, but the tone struck him as warm and reassuring.

Then he realised it was because the men on the other end of the line were the ones they were on their way to rescue. The ones under fire.

He really appreciated those four inches of armour.

CHAPTER FIVE

Taking a break from the cramped confines of the crew compartment, Alexander was standing up on the top of the tank, holding onto the barrel of the main cannon for balance as they drove through the French countryside towards Demetier.

"This whole place is getting stranger and stranger," muttered Franklin.

Inhaling deeply on his cigarette, Alexander had to admit that he knew what the commander was talking about. They hadn't seen any sign of military presence on the road since the land mine incident (which O'Brien had only just stopped grumbling about).

"Feels like we're the only ones out here," he replied.

Franklin shook his head, an unsettled look on his face. "It's not just that. I mean, to be honest with you, Alexander, I was expecting that. This mission was supposed to be an absolute cakewalk. All the Germans are supposed to be absolutely miles away from here by now."

Down below them, O'Brien changed gears, and the buzzing, whistling noise grew louder, forcing Alexander to raise his voice to be heard. "Those Yanks must have run into some, though. What else could they have called in assistance for? Even the French Resistance aren't cavalier enough to get into a firefight with a bunch of Americans. For starters, they'd probably just be absolutely massacred."

Franklin nodded. “Oh, absolutely. Don’t get me wrong, I’m grateful for the Resistance, but they’re not military. I think what’s happened is that a German unit was holed up in this little village - perhaps even only four or five men, perhaps with one of those buzzsaw things.”

The tank rocked a little over a pothole, forcing Alexander to lean a little heavier on the barrel. “Buzzsaws?”

“Yes, ‘Hitler’s Buzzsaw’ the boys call them. Nasty things, apparently. Machine guns, you know. Supposed to be even faster and deadlier than the Bren our boys carry. Belt fed, as well, so it can sit there and belch fire at you all day long. Oh, we’d make short work of it, of course, but then maybe that’s what we’re being called in to do.”

“I wish we had more to go on. I don’t like going in blind.”

“Oh, bloody recon is all shot to hell, old bean. You can’t trust a bloody thing from intelligence. I don’t know they’ve ever really been on the money in all the time I’ve been here.”

Alexander threw his cigarette butt off into the side of the road. He really appreciated that Franklin had such a relaxed command in the tank. It made everyone like him, and when the whole crew liked him, they were much more likely to want to do well by him than if he had been bullying and haranguing them into battle.

Franklin had fallen silent as the tank crested a small rise, and then descended down a little, the ground around them flattening out into what could one day make halfway decent farm land - if it ever stopped having the life bombed out of it. “Mist’s coming on. Hope it doesn’t turn to fog.”

Alexander spotted it, too. Little wisps of white and grey were coiling around the grass on the side of the road. It moved hypnotically, like cigarette smoke coiling around the candlelight of a pub back home. The thought made him homesick and he tried to dismiss it as quickly as he could. “Is that a problem?”

"Depends how thick it gets. It'll be no fun for O'Brien to drive in, and we'll be seen long before we ever see anybody. If it is a German unit we're dealing with-"

He paused at the sound of a distant explosion, which rippled across the fields with a stomach punching thud. Alexander listened too, but no more sounds followed. "Artillery?" he asked.

Franklin nodded. "Yes, but I don't know whose and I don't know how far away."

The silence stretched on, with no further shots fired.

The sun had come down now, just touching the horizon, with evening drawing on fast. The light was turning a blue-black hue, heralding the true coming of nightfall. Alexander didn't particularly relish spending his first night in France embroiled in combat with desperate German troops, but it didn't look as though he was going to be given much of a choice.

The mist was thickening, now, rising to two or three inches above the ground, and beginning to spread across the beaten road in front of them. "Is it worth trying the radio again?" Alexander asked. "Now we're closer we may be able to get a stronger signal from the Americans themselves, rather than going through HQ. They could at least give us some idea of what to expect."

The tank commander raised one arm and pointed off ahead of them. "See there, about two, three miles ahead?"

Alexander squinted through the mist. There were some black, squarish shapes just visible in the distance. "I think so. Is that Demetier?"

"That is - if these maps aren't as unreliable as a German's promise - the village of Demetier," said Franklin, pulling himself fully out of the turret, so that Alexander could pass him. "Yes, please go down below and see if you can rouse them on the blower. Get as much information as you can."

"Yes, sir."

"Thank you, Loader/Operator."

The radio brought nothing but static. He repeated the call for a reply so often that the words started to lose all meaning, becoming little more than a mantra, a beseeching cry. He tried reaching the Americans for a full fifteen minutes before admitting defeat. He relayed his failure to Franklin who waved in acknowledgment, as though he had not been expecting anything different.

He wondered what was stopping the Americans from replying, and feared the worst.

"This fuckin' thing is impossible to drive in the fucking dark," shouted O'Brien, loud enough to be heard over the constant chug-chug-chug of the engine.

"Why don't you put the goddamn lights on, then?" Bright shouted back at him.

"Oh, yeah, that'll do us a world of good. We'll be able to see everything except the Kraut that fired the fucking bazooka at us that killed us. You're a prize moron, you know that, Bright?"

Bright chuckled, his eyes twinkling as he smirked at Alexander. Alexander sensed that there was some long standing friendly rivalry at work. The two men enjoyed riling each other up, but it was actually as a form of affection, rather than a genuine push towards malice. Alexander clambered back to shout up at Franklin. "O'Brien can't see a bloody thing. What do we do?"

"Can't see too much myself, old boy," the commander yelled back. "That mist's getting thicker by the minute."

"We've got to hit the lights," suggested Alexander.

Franklin nodded. "Aye, there's a bridge coming up; we're only about five hundred yards off."

Alexander shuffled and squeezed his way back down the crew compartment of the Comet, awkwardly reached over O'Brien shoulder and switched on the head lamps. Their hooded glow - while pretty dim compared to what they really needed - seemed to instantly increase O'Brien's vision a hundred fold. "That's much better! It was like trying to find a black cat in a dark cellar just a moment ago. Aw, crap, there was a road sign, but I couldn't see it. Too high up. Go ask the commander if it was anything important."

Franklin had already preempted the question and dropped down into the main compartment, buttoning down the turret above him. "That sign said 'Demetier'. That's the village we're looking for. Take it slow and easy, O'Brien. We don't know who's here, or where they may be hidden."

O'Brien had an unlit cigarette in his mouth (even he wouldn't dare light one inside the tank), and was muttering gently and cursing around it at a volume that Alexander assumed only he, and maybe Bright, could hear. "Oh, aye. Don't worry, I'll be driving plenty careful, you fucking posh nancy. Like me driving carefully will make a lick of difference if there's some Hitler Youth arsehole holed up with a fucking Panzerfaust. We'd be brown bread before you had a chance to tell me off for going too fast, you big Jessie."

Alexander tried to avoid smirking. He was pretty sure he was doing a bad job of it, and was grateful for the darkness inside the tank.

The tracks bit into the soft earth, compacting stones down and to the side as the Comet eased its way down the path to the village. The humpback bridge leading across the river was a tight fit for the thirty-two tonne war machine, but O'Brien was an excellent driver, and they made it across without so much as a scratch to their paint work.

Once there, the path opened up again, and O'Brien leaned forward in his seat, trying to make out where to head next. "I don't see the town yet, boys. It could be another couple of miles off. I'll tell you this much, though: no-one's got any lights on. Land like this, you'd be able to see if someone had so much as left a candle burning in a bedroom somewhere."

"Maybe they're in blackout?" Alexander asked. "Could be that they're worried about Stukas, or just drawing the attention of the Germans?"

Cleveland tapped Franklin lightly on the shoulder. "See if you can get the Yanks on the blower. Tell them we need some sort of clue as to their position, verbal or visual, it doesn't really matter. Just see if you can get something out of them."

Franklin nodded. "Good idea."

O'Brien slowed the tank to a stop, the constant chug and grunt of the tank's engine serving as a comforting drone.

"Can you see anything at all?" Alexander asked him, trying to squint through the driver's vision slit.

"The mist's getting thicker. The lamps aren't helping much, you see. It's just glaring back at it, so it's like trying to drive through tobacco smoke. If it were up to me, we'd wait until it was light again, we're just going to end up getting blown up or - if I'm really stupid - getting run aground on something."

"The Americans need our he-"

"The Yanks aren't answering the radio, which means that in all likelihood, they're already dead, killed by whoever's going to end up killing us if we charge in there. I just hope Franklin's got a better plan than I have."

"What's your plan?"

"I don't have one."

Cleveland tapped Alexander on the shoulder. "No news on the radio, so it sounds like if the Yanks are still alive, then they're holed up tight. If they were in a firefight, then you'd think they'd want to get us over there as quickly as possible, so Franklin's saying to shut down for the night. Sleep in the tank, though. No point wandering around in the dark waiting to get shot by the Germans."

O'Brien killed the engine, and the tank fell silent.

After a few minutes of nothing but the wind whistling around the turret, and the breathing of his team mates, Alexander whispered into the darkness, "That's all we do? We just sit here?"

Cleveland's voice came from behind him, "That's what war is, lad. Months of boredom, and minutes of terror."

"If the Americans can get to a radio," said Franklin, "they'll contact us and we'll get out there. In the meantime, sleep while you can."

O'Brien was already snoring, the dull buzz reverberating around the confines of the tank.

"It's going to be a long fucking night," muttered Bright.

Alexander wasn't sure what he had expected from being in a war zone, but he was certain that this had not been a part of it. The stuffy darkness, full of the snores, wheezes and farts of his crew felt truly surreal. He slept fitfully, squeezing his neck at an odd angle to try and get comfortable in his crew position, wedged up against the side armour. Occasional whispers as Cleveland and Franklin conversed quietly broke through his consciousness, and he opened his eyes, only to be greeted with more blackness. What little light there was shone in through small vision slits, and served to illuminate very little indeed.

He came fully awake several hours later, when Franklin threw open the turret hatch, and a pale, grey light tumbled in.

First Franklin, then Cleveland, led the way out of the tank, and he followed, Bright and O'Brien trailing behind him.

The tank stood in a field, the earth chewed up to a muddy pulp by their tracks. The dawn's light was a pale orange, washed out and filtered by the mist that stretched away from them in every direction. Alexander clambered up to the hull of the tank, and then dropped down to the ground, his boots sinking slightly into the dew dampened soil. "It looks like the end of the world," he whispered.

Cleveland nodded, turning on the spot, looking around and around. Some trees were just visible, tall dark monoliths in the mist, their branches reaching out like the ribs of a giant skeleton.

"You hear that?" Bright said, his voice oddly loud in the stillness. He dropped it to a whisper and asked again, "Do you hear that?"

"I don't hear anything," replied O'Brien, lighting a cigarette.

"Exactly," Bright replied. "There's no planes, no artillery, no gunfire. It's not just that, though. There's no birds."

Alexander nodded to himself, reaching out with one hand to grab a hold of the tank, to ground himself against the eerie stillness. "He's right. It's dawn, and there's no birdsong."

He felt his arm hairs rise inside his shirt sleeves, and he fumbled a cigarette out his pack to give his shaking hands something to do. It was just freak weather, of course, but it was plain strange to see. The birds must just be deeper in the trees, and the fog was dampening their sound. Yes, that made sense, didn't it?

"We're never going to find the pigging village in this," muttered O'Brien, idly pulling a clod of earth from the track.

Franklin had been silent since they'd exited the tank, as spellbound as the rest of them, and seemed to physically shake himself out of his reverie. "Nonsense, old bean. A bit of fog isn't going to stop the British army. We have radios, we have maps and we have compasses, don't we? Cleveland, get us a position and get us to Demetier as soon as possible."

"Will do, skip."

"The rest of you, get the tank warmed up and running as quick as we can. I want us moving as soon as possible. You can eat your breakfast on the road."

A chorus of affirmations rose from them all, but to Alexander's ears they seemed flat, deadened by the oppressive atmosphere. He remembered what he'd said upon climbing out of the tank, the words seeming to have come from out of nowhere. "It looks like the end of the world", he had said.

He shivered in the cold and damp, then climbed back into the tank to begin preparations to speed them towards Demetier, and the squad that needed their help.

CHAPTER SIX

The mist remained with them.

Alexander had expected to subside as the rising sun warmed the countryside, or for the gentle winds to disperse it; but the warmth did not seem to affect it, and the wind itself seemed deadened by the constant pall of grey that hung over them.

The Comet made short work of the remaining miles to the village of Demetier, and he felt his heart rise a little as Franklin reported that they'd just passed a signpost for the village. As it approached ten o'clock in the morning, O'Brien reported that he could just make out the dim shapes of buildings in the distance. "Shouldn't be too much longer now, lads."

"What's 'not too much longer'?" Bright called back. "Should we get the kettle on?"

"Save that for after we rescue the American nancy boys," muttered the driver. "Still can't see a fucking thing at the moment. Alexander, get Franklin to try the radio again; we're almost on top of them."

Alexander clapped O'Brien's shoulder in acknowledgment and squeezed his way back to the turret. "Franklin, O'Brien says it may be worth trying the radio again."

"Right-o," Franklin called back down to him. "Why don't you give it a go, then?"

"You mean, I should..?"

"You've used one before right? I don't want to have to come down there as this bloody pea soup is hard enough on O'Brien as it is. I figure he needs all the help he can get - not that he'd ever admit to it, of course."

"Uh...I'll give it a go."

Alexander hadn't used a radio since basic training, and wasn't sure he was doing it right even then. He managed to fumble his way around the talk button and got out a brief message, urging the American squad to get in contact if they heard him, but there was no reply forthcoming. There were occasional burbles and clicks in the static that made his heart jump, thinking it was the start of a message, but there was never any actual communication in its wake.

He reported his failure to Franklin, who waved his acceptance, and returned to the main compartment, similarly reporting the lack of activity to O'Brien.

"Typical. You know what I reckon, lad? I reckon we'll have driven all the way out here to help them, and they'll be long gone. Oh, I don't mean dead, I just mean they'll have managed to escape, and never once thought to report back that the situation has changed, so we're stuck here on a bloody wild goose chase. Typical, eh?"

The noise of the tracks changed abruptly. The steady drone and whistle shifted to more of a staccato rumble.

"Cobblestones," O'Brien said. "I guess that means that we're here."

Franklin yelled down into the tank, barely audible above the engine, but clear enough to Alexander to hear and relay to O'Brien. "Bring us to a stop. This looks like the town square, right enough."

O'Brien - assisted by Alexander - threw levers, stepped on pedals, and eventually brought the tank to a dead stop, finally switching off the engine. They heard the sound of Franklin climbing out of the turret and walking across the hull. The whole crew seemed to be holding its breath in total silence, waiting to hear what the orders were.

Eventually, his steps clanged back across the hull to the turret, where he knocked on it sharply twice, and called "Come on up, chaps. It's a lovely day."

Alexander was the first out, and was more than a little disturbed to discover that the mist had remained and - if anything - was actually a little heavier than he remembered it being early in the morning. He dropped down from the tank onto the cobbled street, looking around for any sign of the squad that had called them down there, but there was none. Truth be told, there was no sign of anyone at all.

"The whole place must be abandoned," he said, squinting through the fog at the dull, lifeless buildings around them.

"That's a dangerous assumption to make," Franklin replied, checking his handgun. "Any of those buildings could contain a sniper, every step could hide a booby trap. It doesn't even have to be German military, remember. All it's got to be is some stupid resistance fighter low on sleep and high on excitement."

"Why don't we stay in the tank, then?" asked Bright, emerging from the Comet behind them.

"Because tanks don't fare too well on a house by house search, which, I'm sad to say, is what it looks like we're going to be doing."

Alexander shivered in the cold, damp air. He didn't like the idea of it any more than Bright, but he didn't want to sound like a complainer, either. He was here to do a job, and he was going to do it well. He unfastened the holster of his own sidearm, and slowly circled around.

His boot skidded a little and he looked down to see what he was standing on.

Spent shell casings.

Squatting, he picked up a few, rolling them in his hand. They didn't look British, that was for sure. "Sir?" he called over to Franklin, forgetting the commander's approach to formality in his nervousness, "what do you make of these?"

He tipped a few of the shell casings into Franklin's open palm, and the commander studied them for a moment, concentration etched across his face. "Looks like machine gun rounds. Nothing that the farmers around here would be using. Certainly doesn't look like something from a Bren gun, or any of ours to be honest."

Cleveland joined them, and picked up another of the rounds from the floor, giving it a quick sniff. "Can't smell any cordite. They've been sat here a while, wherever they came from."

"The fog and rain could have gotten rid of any smell," mused Alexander.

"Maybe. Anyway, I'd guess that's from one of those new German things. A Sturmgewehr Forty-Four, they call it. It's supposed to be all the best bits of a machine gun mashed with all the best bits of a rifle. Great fun to use, but horrible to be at the receiving end of."

"You think there was a firefight, here?" asked Alexander.

"Aye, I do. Those American lads were hiding from something, after all; and the Germans seem the mostly likely culprits, don't they?"

Franklin waved over Bright and O'Brien, the latter already lighting a cigarette and grumbling about the weather or the war or whatever was bothering him most at the time. When they arrived, Franklin once again checked his sidearm and said, "Okay, for whatever reason, it looks like our Yankee friends aren't picking up the telephone. They could be dead, they could be injured, or they could simply be long gone by now. What that means is that we're going to have to go looking for them until we know for sure."

O'Brien started to say something, but Franklin stopped him with a raised hand. "The weather here isn't doing us any favours, of course. So take it easy, take it slow, and for now don't go out of sight of the tank. I want everyone to be able to make it back here in a hurry if they need to."

There was a mumbling of "Aye, sirs", and the crew turned on their heels and began exploring the town.

Cleveland tapped Alexander on the elbow, and smiled. "Come on, lad. You can stick with me."

"All right. Which way do we head?"

"Does it matter? We're in the middle."

They had only taken a few steps before they found the fountain.

Standing eight feet tall, carved with whorls and spirals, foxes and birds, it now stood unmoving, the pumping mechanism apparently having failed sometime in the village's past. What water remained inside was dark and covered in a green film. "Seems a little extravagant for a simple farming village," mused Alexander, tracing one of the designs with a fingertip.

"Maybe when this was put in it was a very different time for the village," suggested Cleveland. "Villages change over the years. It might have been a lot bigger, or a lot richer, back then."

"Maybe."

"If that's the case, then they wouldn't get rid of it. They'd see it as a status symbol and want to keep a hold of it. Especially the Frogs. You know what they're like."

"What do you mean?"

Cleveland shrugged. "You know what I mean. The Frenchies are all a bit up themselves. That's why they eat and drink like wankers, and have you seen that art gallery they've got in Paris? *The Looov*, they call it. Load of rubbish."

"Oh, right. No, I haven't been."

"That'll be why this is somewhat in disrepair, though. They couldn't get rid of it, but they couldn't keep it nice, either."

Alexander looked over his shoulder. The tank was still visible through the mist, although it was already starting to lose detail. He could see Franklin stood up top, keeping a watch for all of them as they explored the village square. He hoped that this part would be over soon, and they could get back on the road, tracks churning up the soil towards the home base. This cold, grey, eeriness was not what he had thought that war would be like. "Think we can go a little further?"

"I should think so. See those buildings there - shops, I dare say - we should still be able to see the Comet from there."

"Right you are."

They walked around the fountain, their boots once again sending some shell casings rolling. "Schmeisser," muttered Cleveland. "Definitely the Germans."

"Not the Americans?"

"No, not unless they found some German weapons."

"Doesn't it concern you there's no sign of them?"

Cleveland shrugged. "Not exactly. As Franklin said, they could be holed up in a building somewhere. If they're commandos or the like, then it's possible that they won't be found until they want to be."

The sound of their footsteps took on an otherworldly quality as they slowly advanced to the buildings on the edge of the village square. Alexander had expected them to echo across the cobblestones; and in a way they did, but it sounded very odd to his ears. It was almost as though the fog was a solid wall and their footsteps were bouncing back at them from a mere ten feet away. The result was every footfall became a rapid rattle of clicks and taps, which made the village seem even more surreal.

The building in front of them was gaining focus now. It was a baker's shop, going on the shelves and damp, mouldy bread in the broken window. The toe of Alexander's boot sent some more shell casings rattling and rolling across the cobblestones. "Must have been one hell of a firefight," he muttered.

Cleveland reached out with one hand and touched a dark red stain on the wall that made Alexander's blood run cold. "Or one hell of a massacre. Just German shells fired, windows shattered...this blood is old, but not so old it's faded completely."

"Where are the villagers?"

"I don't know."

Something made Cleveland straighten up and spin around, raising his gun up high.

Alexander instantly followed suit, straining to see anything through the eddying fog. "What? What is it?"

"Didn't you hear that?"

"I didn't hear anything!" Alexander hissed back at him. "Are you trying to wind me up?"

"I heard...I thought I heard someone singing. A woman."

"I didn't hear anything."

Cleveland lowered his gun a little. "It's gone now. Maybe it was just birdsong. Yes, just the birds."

Alexander didn't say anything, but he hadn't heard a single note of birdsong all day. "What was she singing?"

"It was a song I knew, but...the words weren't quite there. I can't place it."

"You mean the words were different, but you knew the tune?"

Cleveland holstered his pistol. "Yes, I suppose so."

"We should head back. I'll listen out for what you might have heard, but I'll tell you right now: if anyone is here, you can be damned sure that they weren't singing a song and dance about it."

Alexander wondered if he should be calling out, to see if there were any survivors - be they civilian villagers, or the American military they were searching for, but dismissed the thought instantly. If there were any German troops left in the area, then their best chance at survival would be to make as little noise as possible. Instantly, he became hyper-aware of each sound he made, from the tap of his boots on the cobbles, to the susurrus of his trouser legs rubbing as he walked. Even his breathing seemed suddenly and impossibly loud, though he knew that could not be the case.

He could just make out the fountain as a dull, shadowy shape in the fog, and they both trod carefully towards it. The muscles around his eyes felt stretched and tired from straining to see through the mist, his brain interpreting each eddy and swirl as someone ducking away from them, trying not to be seen.

His arm hairs rose as he heard - just on the limits of his awareness - the sound of someone singing.

He stood still, cocking his eye at Cleveland. "Did you hear that?"

"I can hear what sounds like O'Brien grumbling over that way. Is that what you meant?"

"No. I thought...no, it doesn't matter..."

Cleveland studied him curiously. "Did you hear her too?"

Alexander nodded. Yes, he wouldn't have been certain until Cleveland asked him, but it had sounded like a woman. A melancholy, yearning sort of tune, although the words were indistinguishable. "I think so. Just for a moment."

"Perhaps someone has left a jukebox running somewhere. There must be a pub or something hereabouts, surely? Yes, that must be it."

Alexander shivered. "Yes, of course. It's going to drive me potty what the song was, though. I recognised it sure enough."

"Did you catch any of the lyrics?"

"No, I...I don't think that it was in English, you know. It must be a translation or something. Some Frenchie re-recorded it for over here, I suppose."

Cleveland stumbled a little as his boot rolled over another pile of shell casings. "Good lord, how many bullets did these Krauts manage to work their way through. They could have killed everyone in the village, with the amount they went through."

Alexander nodded his assent, and felt his heart lift a little as the shape of the Comet drew into focus. Franklin was still there, too, leaning against the turret. Two glowing red lights at the rear showed where Bright and O'Brien were getting in a crafty cigarette.

The tank and his friends were a sight for his - literally - sore eyes, but it would be a stretch to say that he felt safe. Something felt very strange about the village of Demetier, and he was not a hundred per cent certain that he wanted to find out what it was.

CHAPTER SEVEN

Franklin smiled and raised a hand in acknowledgment as they approached the tank. "Jolly good to see you chaps! Was starting to think that you'd gotten lost for good."

Something in their faces told him that this wasn't something that should be joked about and he instantly sobered. "What did you find?"

Cleveland shucked a cigarette from his packet straight to his lips and lit it, while Alexander reported in. "Not a lot, truth be told. Lots of shell casings. Jerry certainly threw a lot of firepower around here. Some shop windows have been smashed in, most likely by stray bullets, but maybe just through vandalism; maybe a looting, come to think of it. We certainly didn't see anyone alive."

"You mean you found someone dead?" Franklin asked, an eyebrow raising involuntarily.

"We didn't find anybody, sorry to say, skip," interrupted Cleveland. "Nobody here but us chickens; and the fog, of course."

O'Brien and Bright moved closer to join the conversation. O'Brien looked up at the commander. "I say we get out of here. We were called in to assist those Yankee nancy boys, and now it turns out that they're not here after all. I'd say that means that our mission is done and dusted."

Franklin shook his head. "There could be German troops here. There could be injured American troops. There could be civilians in need of assistance. I'm sorry, my friend, but we need to look closer. Take a smoke break, get some lunch inside you, and then we'll have to take another look around."

"This is turning into a proper wild goose chase," O'Brien grumbled, clambering up the side of the tank, and squeezing himself down the turret and inside.

Alexander started eating his lunch on the hull, but the fog began to get to him after a while. He found he was constantly staring into its dizzying depths, or imagining that someone was behind him, or just out of vision, observing the tank and its squad for some devilish reasons of their own. After a few minutes of this, without comment or observation, he joined O'Brien inside the tank, to finish eating his meal. It stank of diesel and lubricant, but at least it felt secure. He felt safe in the tank. He could put his back to something.

O'Brien didn't say a single word to him, and they ate their lunch in silence.

After half an hour or so had elapsed, Franklin banged on the hull to signal the end of the lunch break and they begrudgingly obliged. O'Brien chose this moment to raise a concern, saying that he should stay behind and do some maintenance work on the tank, so perhaps it would be a good idea for Franklin to head out into the fog with the rest of them.

Franklin plastered on a smile, but Alexander knew that this was the one thing that the man had been desperate to avoid. He had been enjoying the safety of the Comet just as much as he had.

The partners were switched, also, to help increase the chance that a new partner might help spot something that the old partner had missed. "A second pair of eyes," Cleveland called it. He took off with Bright in the direction of the fountain and the bakery, which he and Alexander had previously explored. Franklin and Alexander watched them leave, their forms becoming dim shapes and then simply fading entirely much quicker than one would have expected. It was as though the fog dropped a curtain down, completely obfuscating them from view. There was a resounding clang as O'Brien disappeared into the tank, and slammed the main hatch behind himself.

Alexander shifted a little awkwardly, waiting for the commanding officer to decide which way to go.

After what seemed like several minutes, but must only have been seconds, Franklin shivered and looked off in the direction they had been driving when they pulled into Demetier. "Well, we know what's behind us, and the other two have already explored off that way. We'll swing back and cast a second pair of eyes in case they missed anything, but I can't help but wonder if it would be better for us to head straight ahead a little bit, what do you say? We could walk straight into the Yankees that way, and that would make much more sense than messing about in the cold and wet, what?"

Alexander reached into his pocket and pulled out a wool cap his mother had made for him, and stretched it over his head. He could feel beads of moisture from the fog form on it almost instantly, but it kept the chill from his ears, which made him feel instantly more comfortable. "That sounds like a grand idea to me, skip."

Franklin flashed a quick smile and they strode bravely into the fog. Alexander made frequent glances over his shoulder as they went, his heart sinking as the Comet grew gradually less defined, and eventually faded from view.

"I say, that's got to be worth checking out all right, hasn't it?"

Franklin's excited voice caused him to start a little and he snapped his head back to where they were heading. There, only thirty yards or so in front of them, was a church. It seemed to be much larger than a village this size would have required, but he remembered what Cleveland had said about how it was possible the village used to be much bigger and richer than it now was. Much bigger and richer than the war had forced it to become.

"You think the Yanks could be hiding in there, boss?"

"I'd say that if they're still here, then it's probably the best place for them to hide in. Sheltered, warm, likely stocked with supplies, and easy to defend. Put it this way, if I were them, then that's where I'd head to."

The stone building looked almost black in the fog, surrounded by a low drystone wall, with a black, rusted gate set by a short path to the church's main entrance. It looked like something straight out of a gothic novel, and Alexander had to once again suppress a shiver. The fog moved low across the tombstones, sweeping and edging back and forth despite the apparent lack of wind. "It's a spooky place," he whispered, blushing instantly.

"Yes, I suppose it is a bit," said Franklin, "but I suppose that this fog would make anything look a little eerie."

He pushed open the gate, and Alexander was a little disappointed when there was no audible squeal or creak. Once again, he found himself constantly checking all around while they walked up the short pathway to the main church door. He tried to convince himself that it made sound tactical sense to do so - they were in an area where they still suspected the Germans to be operating, after all - but there was more to it than that. He just didn't like being there.

He put his back to the church door and kept watch as Franklin tried the handle. The door was huge, easily eight feet high, dotted with metal studs, and the door handle was a colossal wrought iron thing that had been there three hundred years if it had been there a day.

Franklin seemed to strain for a moment, and then the lock shifted with an echoing noise that was halfway between a click and a bang. The door began to swing inwards, and this time Alexander was greeted with the ominous groan he had been expecting at the gate.

What little light shone in from outside showed a small vestibule, some tall candlesticks and books filled up one side, and another door led into the church proper. Alexander drew his pistol and stepped inside. Franklin followed him, closing and latching the door behind them. Darkness swallowed them for a few seconds until their eyes began to adjust to the gloom a little better. Once they had a vague sense of their surroundings, Alexander shouldered open the door, and then stepped into the main room.

They had emerged at the top end of the church, near the altar, which looked dusty and abandoned, yet all of the paraphernalia was still present - apparently whatever had happened in the rest of the village had left the church untouched. Two rows of five pews spread toward the back of the hall, dotted with cushions and prayer books. The gray light from outside did little to illuminate the stained-glass windows, making their colours feel faded and washed out. Enough light passed through them, however, so the room still felt well-lit.

One thing at the rear of the church struck them as very strange. A small, square table, with a burning candle atop it.

"Someone must be here," whispered Franklin. "Tread carefully. We don't know how receptive they'll be to strangers."

Alexander nodded, thumbed the safety from his pistol, and stepped into the main room, his footsteps echoing around them. The wan light cast strange shadows across the whole of the church, the pews seeming to positively heave with movement, as though a phantom congregation were seated there.

Franklin took the lead, Alexander stepping just behind him, still constantly sweeping back and forth with his pistol, ready to squeeze out a shot at the first sign of something - no, some*one* - leaping from out of the shadows. Each footfall seemed to echo strangely, the sound momentarily sucked into the emptiness around them, then to be spat back at them to scatter this way and that like a flock of disturbed bats.

"Should we call out?" Alexander whispered hoarsely, his throat dry.

Franklin didn't answer, and simply shook his head, stepping forward carefully, his eyes flicking up and down, scanning for any sign of movement.

Eventually, they reached the table, with its single flickering candle. Alexander maintained a vigilant watch, and Franklin stooped forward to examine its contents. "What is it?"

"Bread, cheese, wine...a bible."

"Someone's still living here, then."

Franklin nodded. "I should say so; if you can call this living."

"Could they be German?"

"I don't know. I can't say for certain that they aren't."

They both straightened up instantly, weapons drawn, at the sound of a door opening along the wall nearest them, just a few feet away. The latch sound echoed away into the cavernous room, and the door creaked slowly open.

"Who goes there?" Franklin barked, sighting down his pistol. "This is Lieutenant Oliver Franklin of the British Army. Show yourself."

Alexander was suddenly sweating. He could feel the cold rush of adrenaline surge all across his body to settle in a nauseating puddle in his stomach. The door creaked open a little more, and a thin, French accented voice came forth. "Do not shoot."

Franklin repeated his demand. "Step forward, and be seen."

The door swung in a little further, and a tall, thin man stepped out. He stood a little over six feet tall, and was rather haggard in appearance. A length of stubble on the cusp of becoming a full beard that was in desperate need of trimming, pale hair cropped short, and blue eyes that were beyond tired, the fragile light making them appear sunken into his skull. Lastly, Alexander took in what he was wearing: black robes, and a bright white dog collar.

His voice was heavily accented French. “Please, do not shoot. I am a man of God.”

Alexander lowered his gun, but Franklin kept his trained on the man. “Who else is here?”

The man shrugged, hesitated, them mumbled, “They are all gone.”

“Gone where?”

The man shook his head and shrugged. “You have transport here with you? You did not come on foot, surely?”

Alexander reached out and lowered Franklin’s arm, and met little resistance. “Yes, we have a tank. We’re with the British Army.”

The man seemed to pale a moment, then regained his composure. “A tank? How many are you?”

“Five.”

The man staggered forward, and reached a hand to Alexander’s shoulder, testing that he was a real person and not just some hallucination. A smile crept to the corner of his lips as he realised that they were actually here, ready and willing to aid him. As quickly as it had lit up, his face became grave again, and he looked nervously at them. “Where are the others? Are they in the church?”

“No,” replied Franklin. “Two are exploring the rest of the village, looking for anyone else still alive here. One has remained with the tank, doing some maintenance.”

“Your tank is damaged?”

“No, just some maintenance, so that we can get out of here as soon as possible.”

“That is certainly an excellent idea, but the other two...we must find them as soon as possible. They are in terrible danger all the while they are here.”

“What do you mean?”

“Please, just trust me, there...it is not safe here.”

Franklin grabbed the priest's arm, firmly but not aggressively. "Steady on, old bean. They are trained soldiers in His Majesty's armed forces, and aren't likely to be jumping at shadows or falling head over heels on the cobblestones. Now, how about you slow down and tell us who you are, at least? As we said, I'm Franklin, and this is Alexander. Now...who might you be?"

The man retrieved his arm from Franklin's grip and nodded, contrition on his face. "My name is Basile. Father Basile Geiger."

"Sounds like a German name."

"My family is originally from the German quarter of Switzerland, but I was born in France, and have lived all my life here. I took over as the priest here about two years ago."

Franklin nodded, and offered him a cigarette, which the priest accepted gratefully. He took one for himself and lit both from the same match. "All right, Father. Have you seen or heard any sign of an American unit in the area? That's why we're here, you see. We're looking for them. Sent to aid them, you know."

Geiger shook his head. "No, I haven't seen anyone. I heard some shots fired a couple of days ago, but I'm not a fighting man. I just stayed in my back room there, until it fell quiet. I don't go outside of the church any more, anyway. It is too dangerous out there."

Alexander didn't like how evasive the man was being. "What do you mean, too dangerous? Are the Germans nearby?"

Father Geiger snorted, coughing a little on his cigarette. "No, the Germans are long gone. They disappeared when the fog came."

"So what is there to be scared of out there?"

If Alexander didn't know better, he'd swear that there were the beginnings of tears in the man's eyes. "I don't know. There is something out there, hidden in the fog. And if we do not find your friends soon, then it may find them."

CHAPTER EIGHT

"Oh, finally," Cleveland cried, sarcastically. "At last there's a place to get a drink in this stupid, poxy place!"

The building before them was a spectacularly uninviting, boxy, rectangular edifice, and - judging by the sign hanging life less in the dead air - was the village inn. The glass in the windows looked thick as the bottoms of milk bottles, and the inside was as dark and uninviting as the rest of the square. Bright shivered a little, and peered at the swollen, wooden sign, hanging from a wrought iron brace.

"*L'Agneau Abattu*," he read aloud. "What's that mean?"

"Search me," muttered Cleveland. He took a drag of the cigarette he held reversed in a cupped hand, a method supposed to prevent snipers taking a bead on the little red glow; although Bright suspected that it actually had more to do with not being spotted sneaking a smoke by a commanding officer. "I don't speak a word of that bloody frog language. Diseased tongue. Probably means 'The King's Head'. The French are terrible for decapitating their monarchy, you know. That sort of thing would never fly back home."

Bright thought about educating him, but just sighed. If he wasn't showing an interest in history by now, then he was probably never going to. "Should we take a look inside? I mean, if there's going to be anything of interest anywhere around here, that's where it'll be, right?"

"How do you reckon, old bean?"

Bright shrugged. "Big building. Food and drink in there. Sounds like the perfect place to hold up, to me. Besides, we might run into a bottle of something we can take back to the tank. Make the trip home fly by a little easier. What do you say?"

Cleveland caught his meaning and smiled. "Ah, I'm with you, all right. Okay. Let's see what we can see, shall we?"

He took a hold of the door handle, turned it with a metallic 'clack' and pushed. It didn't budge. "Moisture in the fog must have gotten to it. Wood's swollen up."

Both he and Bright put their shoulders to the door and shoved. After a moment's squeaking protest, the door relented and granted them entrance, swinging open into the darkness of *L'Agneau Abattu*.

"Can't see a bloody thing in here," muttered Cleveland. He struck a match and held it up high, throwing the cluttered bar-room into a morass of dancing and flexing orange tinged shadows. He spotted a candlestick on the table nearest to them and lit it, and then another on the adjacent table. The feeble light did little to penetrate the further reaches of the dark room, but it made the tables near the entrance feel a little homelier.

"Cheery fucking place," said Bright. "Can imagine working your arse off in the vineyard from the crack of dawn, then spending your evenings in this fucking pit."

"Ah, it's probably all right, once you get a bit of a crowd in," replied Cleveland. Bright couldn't tell if the man was being sarcastic or not. "Let's take a bit of a look around...hello! Well, there's something you don't see every day."

He pushed the door back closed a little way and showed Bright what he had discovered.

Hanging on a peg on the back of the inn door was an SS officer's cap.

"Aw, fuck. Guess that seals it. The Germans were here all right, and I'll say they were definitely up to no pigging good. That lot never are...and the SS to boot? What the hell do those wankers have to do with a little village like this?"

Cleveland picked the hat up and examined it, the candlelight making the totenkopf on the brim seem to grin evilly. "Who knows? I've heard they sometimes just stick them in with a squad or two, just to make sure that they're following orders. Jerry seems to be very reluctant to question a command when it comes from one of these fellows. We should take a look around. Who else knows what we might find."

"I'll keep my eyes peeled for a bottle of scotch and an MG-42."

"That's the spirit."

Cleveland took one of the candles and advanced slowly towards the back of the bar, lifting the candle high and low, searching for any clue as to what may have happened to the village of Demetier and its occupants. Perhaps he was hoping to find one of them hiding in the rafters or cowering under a table somewhere. His candle kept him and a small radius around him illuminated, but it wasn't long before there was a gulf of blackness between him and Bright.

Bright grabbed another candle, took a light off of the one by the door, and headed towards the bar. The guttering light made him constantly on edge, fearing that behind every lurching shadow was a Nazi trooper ready to spring forth and finish him off. He leaned up high, and peered down over the bar, half expecting to receive a bayonet in the neck, but there was nothing there besides some glasses, bottles of wine, and a few plates, dirty with grease and old food. Looking further along, he saw that there were several mugs, glasses and bottles standing on the bar top, some half full - or even more than half full - with abandoned drink. "Someone left here in a hurry."

"How do you mean?" Cleveland called back from the rear of the main room.

"No man leaves his drink like this unless it's something very important. Like 'birth of your first born' important. Couple that with the SS chappie leaving his little bonnet behind, and I think that's a pretty safe guess."

Cleveland didn't respond, so Bright stepped behind the bar, grabbing a bottle of wine as he went, his eyes sweeping the high shelves for some decent spirits.

He was halfway along the bar when he saw it.

There, embedded in the bar, sunk into the old, swollen wood about half an inch, was an SS honour dagger. He'd heard tell of the "Ehrendolch" that was supposedly presented to each member of the SS by Heinrich Himmler himself. It had to be at least twelve inches long, and the candlelight made the steel of the blade turn to a golden fire of its own, shining like something from a fairy story. He reached out and ran his hand down the ebony handle, reading the inscription out loud, although faltering more than a little. "Meine Ehre Heißt Treue".

"What?" Cleveland called out to him.

"Nothing, just...reading the label on the wine. As you said earlier, can't make head nor tail of it. It might as well be Greek or whatever."

"Right. Well, keep looking. If there are Germans holed up here then there's a good chance they left more stuff behind. There might be something we can use."

How many of these things could they have made? If he pocketed it now, he'd be in to make a mint once the war was over. Maybe there'd even be a bounty on them.

Of course, part of it was that he just wanted to keep it for himself. It was a truly beautiful knife, and even if he never sold it, even if he never used it, he could just keep it above the mantelpiece back home. The SS Ehrendolch he'd liberated from Demetier, 1945. It'd be a fun thing to show off to his neighbours; a fantastic little war trophy.

He looked up to check that Cleveland had his back to him, then grasped the ebony hilt firmly and wiggled it from the bar. It came out with little protest, and he slipped it into his boot, the steel feeling practically ice cold even through his socks. Thankfully it was a snug fit, and he wasn't going to have to worry about piercing his foot. He tried his best to tuck his trouser leg over the top of it and into his boots, completely concealing his contraband.

"Found anything?" Cleveland asked, turning back around just as Bright straightened up.

"No, nothing. Can't even find a halfway decent whiskey here. Just wine, wine and more wine."

"What did you expect from a Frenchie village way out in the wilderness like this?"

Bright jiggled his boot a little to make certain that the knife wasn't going to come loose. "I don't know. A little class and taste?"

"This is a ghost town. Come on, let's get out of here."

"Right you are."

Checking once again that the hilt of the Ehrendolch was completely covered, he shuffled awkwardly from behind the bar and waited for Cleveland at the door. Cleveland shouldered the door open, blew out their candles and left them back on the table nearest the door.

Once they were back outside, the pale grey light from the fog blighted square seemed positively dazzling compared to the darkness of *L'Agneau Abattu* and Bright caught himself actually blinking a little. "So what do we do now?"

"Try a little further along, or head back to the Comet?"

"How long were we inside there?"

Cleveland looked at his watch. "We left the tank about twenty minutes ago."

"Seems a shame to call off the trip so early, and we'll only have to put up with O'Brien being a fucking dullard."

Cleveland shrugged, and gestured down the street. "Onwards, then, old boy."

Something snatched at Bright's attention all of a sudden. Something just on the edge of his hearing. He paused, and turned around, looking for the source of the noise, but - of course - all he could see was a wall of fog. "Did you hear that?"

"Hear what?"

Bright could feel adrenaline chugging through his system. "I don't quite know. Something just...it sort of caught my ear I suppose. I thought it was someone...someone singing."

Cleveland pointed up to where the sign for *L'Agneau Abattu* was swinging slightly. "Could it have been that, old boy? Swinging in the breeze? That old bracket looks pretty rusty."

Bright was unconvinced. "I don't know. Possibly; but there doesn't seem to be any..."

He looked back up, his arm hairs rising. The sign had stopped moving.

"...wind."

Cleveland had noticed it, too. "Maybe we should get back to the tank, don't you think? O'Brien might be in need of a hand after all."

Bright nodded. Any excuse. Any reason. "Yeah, I reckon you're right. Back that way wasn't it?"

Cleveland had already started to walk. "That's it, follow me."

Then he heard the sound again. A woman singing, low.

"Shit, Cleveland, do you hear that?"

Cleveland had sped up his pace, and was already ten yards away from him, fading into the fog, which seemed to be eddying and swirling around him, cutting him off from view.

"Cleveland! Slow down! I can't see you!"

It was obvious that Cleveland had heard him, as the officer slowed down, turning back over his shoulder to look for him, but it was as though the fog was thickening. Bright picked up his pace to catch up, but with each step, it seemed as though Cleveland was disappearing deeper into the fog, until he was just a shadowy form, and then completely faded from view.

Bright's heart sank, and he realised he was lost in the fog of Demetier.

He stopped for a moment, spinning on his heels, trying to get some sense of where he might be in relation to *L'Agneau Abattu*, the tank or even the fountain. There was nothing to be seen. The fog seemed to be growing if not heavier, then *denser*, even the sound of his own breathing appeared to echo back to him from less than ten feet away. "Cleveland!" he shouted again, straining his ears for any sound of him calling back.

They'd been walking in a straight line, hadn't they? Surely if he just retraced his steps, he'd bump into the pub again. Yes, that made sense. He could wait it out there until either they came to find him, or the fog dissipated. Once the fog cleared, he'd probably find he was less than a hundred yards from the tank. They'd rib him endlessly about it afterwards of course, but he could put up with that if it meant he could get out of the grey purgatory that surrounded him.

He didn't exactly relish the idea of spending the night in that dark inn, either, but at least it would be out of the chill, and he could dig deeper, see if he could light a few candles, or maybe even get a fire started. A place like that would have a lovely great fireplace, and he could have it all to himself.

Maybe there'd be some more Nazi treasure to be found, as well. He'd have the best mantelpiece on the street.

A snatch of song reverberated through the fog toward him. The melody was familiar, but the lyrics seemed guttural, littered with hard consonants.

German.

He snatched his pistol from his belt, and held it ready, spinning back and forth, watching for any sign of movement in the fog. "Who goes there?"

The voice came again, a contralto on the edge of hearing.

"Who goes there?" Bright practically screamed into the fog, his voice coming out in a much higher register than he had anticipated.

There, on the edge of his vision, movement in the fog. A figure just stepping around behind him, moving as if to sneak up behind him. In a panic, his boot skidded on the cobblestones and he went down hard onto the floor. He scrabbled onto his back as quickly as he could, raising the revolver once more, and squinted through the fog. There was no sign of the figure he had seen.

"Cleveland, is that you?"

He was yelling now, struggling to keep the panic from edging into his voice. "Franklin? Alexander? O'Brien? Can any of you hear me?"

Surely he had to be by the pub by now?

He clambered awkwardly to his feet, keeping the pistol at arms length, his eyes aching from trying to peer into the thick, grey clouds. "Are any of you fuckers out there?"

When a figure grew into focus in the fog in front of him, he didn't know whether to feel relieved, or even more nervous than before. Blinking back tears of pure fear, he aimed his pistol at the man, and positively shrieked "Who goes there? Cleveland, speak up or I'll open fire, I fucking swear it!"

The man must only be ten yards from him by now, but he remained completely obscured by the fog. Then Bright became aware of two more men behind him. "Who the fuck are you?"

More shapes, more people. It seemed as though a veritable army was growing out of the fog, and not just in front of him now. They came from the sides, too.

He squeezed off three rounds blindly into the fog, yet still they kept coming, walking slowly toward him.

Something slammed into him from behind, and he fell awkwardly at the feet of the mob.

His final scream did not penetrate the fog.

CHAPTER NINE

"What do you mean, you bloody lost him?" Franklin barked.

"Just what I said, skip. He was right behind me when we left the inn. I could hear him saying something, so I turned back and - poof - he was gone."

O'Brien butted in from the main hatch of the tank, half in and half out of the Comet. "Did you go looking for him?"

"No, I didn't, and I don't regret it. If I went wandering off on my own looking for him, then there's a better than even chance I'd have wound up missing as well. I thought it better I rendezvous here and we can go off together. Now, before we do that...who's this chap?"

Franklin indicated the man they'd found in the church. "This is Father Geiger, the village priest. He thinks there's something funny going on around here."

"I don't think it, Mr. Franklin, I know it. I've seen far too many men go missing, just like your friend has. This is what happens. The fog gets thicker, and thicker, and people are simply gone. Sometimes, if they're very close by, you can hear their screams, but not often. Mostly they are just gone. The Germans who came all disappeared in the fog. The Americans who came after them also vanished in the same way. Now, if we do not get out of this cursed village, then you and your tank will disappear in the exact same way."

They all fell silent for a moment.

"Well, that's a cheery fucking story," muttered O'Brien, lighting a cigarette.

Franklin looked sympathetically at Geiger. "Father, I sympathise with your panic, I really do, but I don't believe that there's anything dangerous about some fog. In any event, we're not leaving until we find Bright."

The priest rubbed his eyes tiredly, and slumped against the side of the tank. "You are wasting time."

"Be that as it may, I'm not leaving him here alone. O'Brien, how goes the maintenance?"

O'Brien shrugged. "Ah, it's all done. I mean, it's much warmer in the tank, so I'd rather stay here but...if young Bright's missing I'll go look for him."

"Two of us should stay by the tank, and two should go search. Don't be longer than twenty minutes. Stay close."

"Right you are, skip."

"Take Alexander. Cleveland and I will wait here with Father Geiger. Maybe you should go check out that inn. If I were in Bright's shoes, then I'd find somewhere to hide out, and if there was something as welcoming as an inn, that'd be my first choice."

O'Brien nodded, and he and Alexander wandered off into the fog.

"You don't think there's something chemical to the fog, do you?" Cleveland asked.

Franklin was sceptical. "How do you mean?"

"Well, I know they say that the Germans promised not to use gas attacks, but can we actually trust them? I mean, who monitors that kind of thing?"

"I certainly don't think it's mustard or chlorine gas or anything like that, if that's what you mean."

"Can you be sure? We don't carry filtration masks, so if you're wrong, who knows what we could wind up suffering with."

The priest chuckled. “The Germans have many flaws, of that there is no doubt, but there are no chemicals in the air, here. They gave their word.”

“So what did happen to the villagers, Father?” Cleveland asked. “And even more intriguingly, how did you manage to get away?”

The priest shrugged. “The fog took them all. And me...I hid.”

***

“Bright, you fucking moron, where are you?” O’Brien hollered through cupped hands.

“You know if there are Germans here that’s going to bring them right down on us. If there’s a sniper in the area, you won’t even bloody know about it.”

Alexander was starting to find the cocksure and cantankerous driver a little grating. He had an abrasive personality at the best of times, but after a day of being cooped up in a noisy tank with him, he was beginning to long for a break.

“Oh, please. There’s not a sniper in the German army - or any army for that matter - who’d be able to draw a bead through this bloody pea souper. I can’t see more than twenty yards, and that’s only if I really bloody squint.”

He wasn’t wrong. Alexander had never seen fog like it, even when he’d worked some early mornings and late nights in London, where the Thames and all the coal smoke supposedly contributed to some really severe fog. “All right, maybe not a sniper, but...they’ve only got to lob one of those bloody stick grenades, and I’d be a goner as well.”

“Well, how else are we going to find Bright?”

“Like Franklin said, he’s probably hiding in the pub with a bottle of whiskey he’s managed to squirrel away.”

“How much further is it to this bloody pub?”

They had come to a stop in front of a butcher's shop. Like all the other establishments they had encountered, this one had all of its windows broken in, and a smattering of shell casings on the ground outside. Here, the bullets had also smashed into the meat in the display area, spattering gore and viscera up the walls and across the floor.

O'Brien gagged and folded his arm around his face, covering his nose and mouth with his elbow. "Aw, fuck. There's a stench and no mistake."

"I'm surprised it's not worse."

"I'm glad it's not fucking worse!"

Wisps of the fog trailed cold, dead fingers over the broken shards at the bottom of the window, and rolled over the trays of meat. Something substantial sat at the back of the display, obscured in shadow and fog. "What is that?" he whispered.

"What's what?"

"There's something at the back there."

"You can go take a look if you want, lad, but I'm staying right here!"

Alexander smirked at the older man, obviously insinuating that he was simply chicken, but O'Brien refused to budge.

His boots seemed deafeningly loud as he approached the window. Glass crunched underfoot, shell casings skittered away from his tread. He raised his pistol to the darkness in the butcher's shop. For all he knew German troops could be hiding inside, ready to let rip at him with a volley of machine gun fire.

He slowed a little, risking a quick glance over his shoulder at O'Brien, who was still watching him incredulously, nose and mouth covered against the smell. Tendrils of fog were snaking over the cobblestones, up and over his boots and ankles. Alexander thought it was amazing that he was only a matter of feet away from the river, yet the fog was already threatening to obscure him from view. He remembered what Cleveland had said about the fog dropping around Bright, and was suddenly fearful of the butcher's shop. He lowered his gun, turned back to O'Brien and stepped to him. "Ah, it doesn't matter. I'm sure it's nothing. It's not Bright, that's for sure."

"Why the sudden change of heart? You were all ready to go in and check out that hidden treasure a second ago."

"It doesn't matter. We should keep looking for the pub. That's where Bright's going to be, if he's anywhere."

"Ah, you pansy. Hold on."

O'Brien pushed open the doors to the butcher's and strode in. Alexander went to follow him, but the older man just shouted at him to wait. After a few seconds, his voice came again, much more enthusiastically this time. "Ah, Alexander, my boy! You were right! It's a heap of buried fucking treasure. We're going to be rich."

"Stop fucking about," Alexander hissed back at him. "Stop making so much bloody noise, and all. You're going to bring a fucking Panzer battalion down on us at this rate!"

"Here, lad! Catch!"

"What?"

Something large - much larger than a football - came hurtling out of the broken window, and Alexander flinched, throwing himself out of its path. "Jesus Christ, O'Brien!"

The missile landed with a wet thud on the cobblestones, and Alexander let out another yelp. "Oh, fuck off, Nicholas; that's disgusting."

There, slack jawed and dead eyed on the cobblestones, covered in green patches of mould and red traces of dried blood, was a whole pig's head.

O'Brien came out of the butcher's shop, laughing to himself, and clapped Alexander on the shoulder. "Oh, man. That was worth it to see your face. Now, come on. Let's find that wanker, Bright."

Alexander was still staring at the pig's head. "You are going to wash your hands before you eat anything, aren't you?"

O'Brien clapped him on the shoulder again, firmly this time, a gesture of warning rather than comfort. He raised his pistol and gazed into the fog. "You hear that?"

Alexander listened for a second, but heard nothing. "No."

"I thought I heard footsteps," grumbled the driver. "This place is going to be enough to make us all go crazy, you mark my words."

"I don't hear anything. Maybe I need to get my ears checked when we get back. Cleveland said he could hear a woman singing while we were at the bakery, earlier."

"It's stopped now, right enough. I just thought...for a moment I thought that I heard someone running along the cobblestones, but there's something about the sound here. It throws you out."

Alexander nodded. "Maybe it's the fog."

"How do you mean?"

"All the moisture in the air. It's got to have some sort of effect on sound, right? Maybe it makes it echo more; or less, for that matter. I don't really know."

"It's a pain in the arse, that's what it is. I've never seen anything like it. It's like we're inside a fucking cloud, you know. Hold! There they go again!"

"What?"

"The footsteps, you fucking clod! Can't you hear them? Bright! Is that you, lad?"

Alexander, wide-eyed, quickly shushed him. "Shut up, you fool. There might still be Germans here! You go shouting like that and you're going to get them all opening fire on us!"

"Oh, fuck off. You think any of them will be able to get a sight of us through this goddamned fog? Jerry's only human, you know. HE's going to be just as bloody put out by all of this as we are."

"Still, please, reign it in a bit."

There was a moment of silence, which O'Brien broke. "It didn't sound like Bright, anyway. It didn't sound like Jerry, neither."

"How do you mean?"

"I...I thought it was a child. There was a sense that it was, I don't know, almost skipping. You know how you can just tell, right? It sounds small, and...I thought it was a child."

"There can't be a child living alone, here, surely?"

O'Brien shrugged. "Could be. If the Germans killed his parents, and he - or she - happened to be hiding."

"I didn't hear anything."

O'Brien shivered, and Alexander realised that this was the closest he'd ever seen the man come to being rattled. Even when they'd rolled over the land mine and had the track blown from under them, he'd been...annoyed, for sure...but he hadn't actually been scared. Now, in the fog blighted village, something was bothering him. It passed in a moment, and the moody, grumpy tank driver re-emerged. "Ah, I must have been imagining it; and even if I wasn't, then there's nothing I do about the poor little thing now. Maybe we can keep our eyes peeled when this fog lifts."

"For sure. Of course we can."

His gaze fell once more on the rotting pig's head. "Let's get on and try and find Bright. We're not getting any closer by standing here nattering. Stupid bastard's probably holed up in the inn, and we can't bloody find it."

Alexander shivered. "We can't just go running off wildly, though, we'll just end up cut completely off from the tank, and having to hole up in a building when this lifts, just like everyone else: Bright, the Germans, your phantom boy..."

His arm hairs rose. Why had he said 'phantom'? O'Brien didn't acknowledge his choice of words, but there was a moment there where a look passed between them, and he nodded. "Aye, you're right. There's no sense in it. Let's head back to the Comet, and just report in. Maybe that priest chap they found has some idea of how to get to the inn. He's been here longer than us, if nothing else."

They headed back in the direction they had come and soon found the fountain. The fog seemed to be trailing a lazy arm over the surface of the water, swirling and cascading over the stonework.

"Hey, what's that?" O'Brien asked.

"What's what?"

"There, there's something in the water, don't you see it? There!"

There was something laying half submerged in the fountain, and Alexander couldn't rightly make out what it was until he reached a hand in and pulled it out. For a moment he had a vision of the rancid pig's heart in the darkness of the butcher's and his stomach turned. His hand met cold thin metal, however, and he pulled the dead weight from the fountain.

Half a pint of fetid, green water spilled out and he held it up. "Well, if we weren't sure before, then we know for sure now: Jerry's involved here, right enough."

It was a German infantry helmet, pitted and scratched, but still intact.

"No. No, that doesn't make sense. Why would he leave his helmet floating in a goddamned fountain, Alexander?"

"Maybe he was killed here."

"The Americans maybe?"

Alexander shrugged and placed the helmet on the floor. Dropping it seemed disrespectful, and putting it back in the fountain even more so. "Probably. Though maybe one of the villagers here took him out. Sniped with a hunting rifle, maybe, or more likely blown away with a farmer's shotgun. Then his friends took the body away."

"Or they left it here. It could be ten yards away and we'd not see it."

That was a chilling thought. The fog was eerie enough without adding in the chance of stumbling across rotting bodies hidden in its dark clouds. "You're a cheery sort today, O'Brien."

"Well, I have to be. You lot are all so pigging miserable, it's up to me to be a ray of fucking sunshine, isn't it?"

"I think that's the tank, there. You see it?"

"The dark splodge in the fog? Yeah, lad, I see it."

CHAPTER TEN

Father Geiger accepted a cigarette gratefully and huddled into his jacket. The temperature was growing colder quickly, and Franklin found himself wondering what sort of time it was likely to get dark around Demetier. He lit a cigarette of his own and asked the priest, “So, Father, perhaps you can shed some light on a little mystery for us.”

“You want to know what happened here?”

“Naturally. To us, this seems to be something of a *Marie Celeste*.”

“I already told you. There is something in a fog.”

Cleveland, standing behind Franklin, rolled his eyes. “Yes, but you seem very unwilling - or, at least, unable - to elaborate on that point. What exactly is it that you think we should be afraid of out here?”

“Captain...”

“Lieutenant.”

“Lieutenant, what do you want me to tell you? You would not believe the truth if I did.”

Franklin stared him down. “Indulge me.”

The priest held his gaze, then sighed. “The fog descended a few days ago, and its first victims were a squad of German soldiers - led by an SS officer - who had wandered into town. They claimed that they were looking for active members of the resistance and, I am sad to report that they tried to arrest and even ended up killing three of the villagers. Two men and a woman. It was a very unfortunate event.

"That night, as the Germans held the town under some sort of martial law - as much as ten men can hold a whole village hostage - they helped themselves to food and drink and tobacco. They had a very good party indeed."

"That sounds like the Nazis, all right," interrupted Cleveland. "Any excuse to have a good old plunder. They're not far removed from those Viking ancestors of theirs, you know."

"The Vikings are from Norway," replied Father Geiger.

"Oh, you know what I meant..."

"I'm sorry, but is this really important?" Franklin asked, desperate to keep the conversation on track. "Why the sudden interest in ancestry? Father, what happened to the Germans?"

The priest hesitated for a moment, and then shrugged. "They left the inn, and walked out into the village square while it was shrouded in fog. I was in church that night, as I thought there may be some of the villagers visiting late and in need of solace, given the unfortunate and terrifying events of the day. As it was, though, I had no visitors that night.

"The first scream came around ten o'clock, and then came the gunfire and the shouting. The Germans sounded panicked; hysterical even. They were running all around, yelling for one another and firing their guns into the air. Then the cries gradually died off, the shooting stopped, and I assumed that their little party had simply finished.

"The following morning, I went for a walk in the village, still expecting everyone to be under their foul jackboots, and was instead greeted by the sight of the villagers gathered around the village square. They said they'd found some bloody marks by the fountain, and by the entrance to the inn, but..."

"What ho, lads!" O'Brien called, trailed by Alexander, gradually growing into focus as they emerged from the fog.

Franklin scowled. "No sign of Bright, I take it?"

O'Brien shook his head. "None. The boy's gone to ground, I reckon. As you said, best guess is that he's curled up in that pub you said that he found. Probably got a nice roaring fire going and everything."

Cleveland raised an eyebrow. "You didn't think to check *L'Agneau Abattu*? Why on earth not?"

Alexander spoke up. "We couldn't find the bloody place. It's the fog, no doubt, messing with our sense of direction. We wound up in some part of the square we'd not seen before. We found a butcher's shop, but there's nothing of use in there, and no sign of the rest of the villagers, for that matter. All we found was a German helmet, discarded, in the fountain. Then we came back here."

"Why back so soon?"

Franklin raised a hand. "They did right. If they were getting concerned enough with getting turned about between here and the inn, then they did the right thing in coming back to the tank. The last thing I want is to lose two men when they were already looking for another."

Father Geiger flung his cigarette butt to the floor, where it fizzled on the damp cobblestones. "Your friend is already dead, or dragged off to wherever this accursed fog takes the people it claims. We need to get out of here as soon as possible."

"We are not leaving here without Stephen Bright. If you want to come with us, then you'll help us find him."

"You cannot find him. Please, Lieutenant, I beg you to get us away from this village! The sooner we break free of this curse, the safer we will all be. The longer we remain, then the sooner we will die!"

No-one responded for a moment, and Geiger's expression of mania gradually faded to one of embarrassment. "I'm sorry, Lieutenant Franklin. Forgive me. It is just...this place has been all I have known for so long. It is getting to me. Getting under my skin.

I have been living in fear of this fog for what seems like a lifetime."

Franklin nodded. "Your apology is accepted, but I will not be leaving here while there is a chance that Bright needs us, or indeed as long as I suspect that he is alive. I will, however, take on board part of your wishes. We will move the tank."

"Sir?" Alexander asked, quizzically.

"'If the mountain will not come to Mohammed', my friend. If we are concerned about getting separated from the tank by moving too far into the fog, then the simple answer is to move the tank deeper into the village. We can trundle forward a hundred yards or so, and widen up our search area considerably, don't you agree? Personally, I think it's a fantastic plan."

Cleveland appeared unconvinced, but said nothing. O'Brien grumbled, and kicked at the cobblestones. Only Alexander was brave enough to venture a counter suggestion. "Franklin, are you sure you want to do that? Visibility in that thing is bad enough as it is without throwing in this fog. Doesn't it make more sense to wait out here until it disperses."

Father Geiger laughed. "It never 'disperses', my son. This fog has been here for three weeks or more, now. Ever since the Germans came."

Franklin scoffed now. "Oh, come now. This is getting altogether too much. I enjoy a ghost story by the fireside on Christmas Eve as much as anyone else but, dash it all, this is neither the time nor the place for it. Father, you are welcome to stay here, walk alongside, or come for a ride in the tank, but we *are* moving, and I will brook no arguments, do I make myself clear?"

O'Brien - not even bothering to grumble this time - pulled himself up the side of the tank, and Alexander followed him. In just a few moments, the engine whirred and choked, yet refused to start. Franklin could hear O'Brien cursing through the viewing slit in front of the driver's seat, and it was enough to turn the air a pretty shade of blue. Again the engine rattled and coughed, refusing to turn over. He revved it for a little longer this time, then abated, wary of flooding the engine.

A few seconds later, Alexander emerged from the main hatch in the turret. “It won’t turn over, skip. We’re trying to figure out why.”

“Don’t you see?” Father Geiger grabbed a hold of Franklin’s sleeve, tugging plaintively. “The fog. It doesn’t want to let us escape. All who have entered this village are cursed, now.”

Franklin felt a little repulsed by the man’s sudden panic and pushed him firmly - though not roughly - away from him, causing him to stumble against the hull of the tank. “Quit talking nonsense, man. I don’t believe that there’s any danger in this fog, unless you count banging your shin on something because you’re not looking hard enough. Bright is likely in the bloody boozer, and as for the Comet...well, there are all sorts of things that can go wrong with a tank, you know. Bits and bobs and crankshafts and levers and doodads and pistons and...all sorts of bloody stuff that I don’t understand. Our man O’Brien there will sort it all out and we’ll be moving just as soon as he gets his hands on it, you’ll see.”

O’Brien emerged from the hatch. “Lieutenant Franklin? The tank’s fucked.”

Father Geiger and Cleveland exchanged a glance, but neither smiled.

Bright climbed up the hull and approached the driver. “What do you mean? Can’t you be a little more specific and a little less foul mouthed?”

O’Brien looked contrite. “Sorry, Franklin. It’s just...I...I don’t have a clue what’s causing it. It just spins and spins and yet there’s no ignition. It’s like the engine just won’t catch. I can try having a nose about with what I can access and the tools I have, but it could be a big job. It could be a really big job.”

“And I suppose the radio is still not co-operating?”

O'Brien shrugged. "We haven't yet tried, skip. We wanted you to know first, but given how our luck is running so far, I'd say there's a very good chance that we won't be able to get a message out of this village, no, sir."

"This day is turning into a bit of a no-hoper, isn't it?"

"As you say."

Father Geiger yelled up at them from the ground. "It's no use us sitting out here, exposed. If your English tank won't move then we should get inside. It's the only way of keeping safe from the fog. Anywhere the fog can get in, it can take people. You need to be indoors. Please!"

"What do you suggest, Father?" Cleveland cut in. "Should we go and take shelter in your church? It seems to me very strange that you somehow managed to avoid this 'Demonic Fog' of yours, yet no-one else seems to have. You say it came for the Germans. Okay, I'll follow along for that part of your story. Answer me this, though: if it came to enact vengeance on the Germans for what they did to a few of your villagers, what then happened to the rest of them?"

The priest shuffled his feet nervously. "It came back."

"The fog. Your demonic fog that avenges the blood of the innocent came back...and did what exactly?"

"I don't understand it myself. It just seemed to be that one night, the fog descended and once again I was hearing screaming all night long."

"And you stayed hidden in your little church."

"Please, Mr. Cleveland, I am not a warrior, and I do not even claim to be a very brave man. Yes, I hid. I am not proud of it and it will haunt me until the day of my judgment but it is what it is. I fell asleep at some point after the screaming stopped. I had been scared that the Germans had come back, but no, as soon as I came out of the door of the church I saw this lifeless fog everywhere. I explored where I could, and found neither hide nor hair of man nor beast.

"It seemed as though the fog was doing something to my sense of direction, also. I was forever getting turned around and ending up in streets that should have been on the other side of the village, or ending up at the same shop three times in as many minutes. I stumbled into a food store and loaded up a handcart with food and drink, which I took back to the church, although that in itself was a nightmare of wrong turnings and confusion. I must have spent a couple of hours travelling a distance of well under a mile."

"And you didn't think to try and escape the village on foot?"

The priest shrugged. "No. No, I didn't. I just got scared again whenever I thought of it. Besides, I assumed that if I had made a break for it, then all that would have happened would have been that I'd have found myself back in the church in an hour or two; or perhaps even worse, I would tire myself out walking and end up just approaching the village from another angle."

O'Brien scoffed. "I'll be below, seeing if I can figure out what the problem is. I'll get us moving, don't worry."

He dropped back down the hatch to the accompaniment of a few yattering bangs and clangs, and after a few seconds, Alexander emerged from the hatch and climbed out onto the hull. "I don't know what you said to him, but he's grumbling like I've never seen him grumble before."

"I didn't say anything," replied Franklin. "It was our Father, here. Seems he thinks that the fog is responsible for the villagers going missing, and for all the Germans, and - I presume - for the Americans, too."

"I say, that is a good point," cut in Cleveland, cocking his head at the priest. "What happened to the Yanks that came through here?"

"Yanks?" asked Geiger, confused.

"Yes, you know Septic Tanks. Americans. Ungrateful Colonials. We got a radio message from an American squad that had wandered into Demetier, and by all accounts they seemed to be having a spot of bother. We were supposed to be their assistance. Then we turn up here, and well - as you say it's been a little strange."

"I didn't hear anything, and I didn't see any sign of them."

"Doesn't that strike you as a little unusual? A deathly silent village and you don't hear ten Americans marching past on cobblestones? Americans being what they are, they probably fired off their guns at everything in sight, too...but you heard nothing."

Father Geiger shrugged. "I heard nothing, as you say. The fog can have unusual effects on sound, though. Sound doesn't travel like it should, here. It's very strange. It is all very strange."

A few minutes passed in silence; or at least as near to silence as could be achieved with a very angry O'Brien banging and cursing inside a thirty-two tonne tank. Eventually, the banging stopped, and then the tank tried to start its engine once again. The engine rattled and wheezed and strained, but refused to turn over.

O'Brien emerged from the main hatch, dirty and sweating. "It's not good. There's nothing bloody wrong with it. I've checked it all over - as near as I can get to all of it, anyway, and the bastard thing...there's nothing wrong with it. It just won't fire up."

CHAPTER ELEVEN

"Well, that just about settles it, doesn't it?" Franklin spat, disgustedly. "We're stuck here until the fog lifts, or until the radio decides to miraculously work, or until the engine suddenly decides it wants to play ball and lets us out of here after all. What a stinking run of luck."

"Luck plays no part in this," muttered Father Geiger. "We are all dead if we do not get back inside."

Franklin sighed. "Look, if you're so desperate to hide from this blasted fog, why don't you get in the bloody tank and help O'Brien out."

"I don't need his blinking help," came a muffled voice from inside the tank.

"You speak when you're spoken to, O'Brien."

"Yes, sir."

Cleveland held up a hand, and cocked an ear into the fog. "You hear that?"

The crew - and the priest - all fell silent, gazing into the fog. It was, once more, like looking into a solid wall of washed out grey. Details blurred and were lost in the constant shifting and eddying of its clouds.

"I thought I heard footsteps," Cleveland spoke up again, "but they've stopped now. A woman's footsteps, I thought. They sounded like high heels, only that's no guide in this fog. Everything echoes, but it also all feels so dead at the same time. It's like whispering into a cathedral. It resonates, but doesn't actually sound far away. It's very strange. Very strange indeed."

Alexander knew exactly what he meant, and had noticed it several times already since they had been there. "It's the water in the air, I think. It muffles everything, and then you've got this big, old empty space full of cobbles and dead buildings and broken glass. It's very strange, all right. You don't know where you are or where anything should be."

Franklin was still listening out, ignoring their conversation. "I don't hear anything."

"That's part of it," said Alexander. "There's no noise at all, is there? Normally you'd at least hear birds chirping, people chatting, or even just the buzzing of flies and bees. There's nothing here, though. It's as close to total emptiness as I've ever experienced."

Franklin hesitated, then smirked. "You two are trying to put me on, aren't you? Playing up to the Father's stories, eh? Well, okay. You got me. I'm spooked, all right? Now, how about you two go off and see if you can find Bright, again, eh? Don't wander too far from the tank though. Stay in visual if you can."

"I say, didn't we just leave this party?" Cleveland chuckled. "Come on, Alexander. Let's go see what we can find this time. Which way was the pub from here? Can you remember?"

"It doesn't matter where you walk."

The priest's voice was like the grinding of stones.

"It doesn't matter where you search, and it doesn't matter how long you walk for. You'll get where the fog wants you to go when the fog wants you to get there."

Cleveland raised an eyebrow and smirked. "Well, Father, there's a little thing called a compass in my pocket, and I think that may well stand to prove you wrong, this time. Come on, Alexander. We'll grab a bottle at *L'Agneau Abattu*, and catch up with these fine fellows afterwards. Cheerio."

"Right you are, sir." Alexander nodded, patting his holster to check that his sidearm was still there.

***

It seemed that they had only been walking for a few feet when they suddenly found themselves directly outside the doors of *L'Agneau Abattu.*

"This doesn't make any sense," breathed Alexander. "We didn't leave the tank but a few seconds ago, it should be right behind..."

He trailed off. The tank was invisible, lost behind a wall of fog that seemed to have become even denser than it had been previously. "Oh, fuck. Cleveland, the tank's gone."

Cleveland span around on the spot. "That can't be. It's got to be right there. I thought I could still hear Franklin talking to that rotten priest...but I can't hear anything now."

"We didn't even walk past the fountain. We've passed the fountain every time. That thing can't be more than ten yards from the bloody tank. How the hell have we got here in about twenty paces, without walking past the bloody fountain?"

"I don't know, but didn't Father Geiger say that stuff like that happens around here? I'm sure he did."

"I don't remember," said Alexander, still squinting into the fog for the missing Comet. "Where the hell can it be?"

"I think you were inside the tank at the time. He definitely said something about how the fog messes around with your sense of direction. Makes you lose all sense of distance and everything. That's what makes me wonder if it isn't some chemical weapon of the Nazis, you know. I know all sides agreed not to use gas after what happened in the last war, but, well, I wouldn't trust Hitler or Albert Speer as far as I could throw them."

"We're pretty stuffed if it is."

"Well, it's definitely non-lethal. We'd all be dead by now, if it were."

"Maybe it's slow acting." Alexander's eyes grew wide. "Maybe that's what happened to the rest of the village."

"If that were the case, then we'd have stumbled across a hundred bodies or more, by now. Look, we can't establish how toxic this stuff might be anyway, so let's not worry about it. We're here now, so let's just take a look inside the inn and see if we can find Bright. If I know that lazy little blighter he's probably already asleep in front of the fire."

Cleveland turned the handle on the door, put his shoulder to it, and shoved inside. He picked up the candle from where he'd left it on the table by the entrance, lit it with a match fumbled from a box in his pocket, and called out, "Bright? Are you in here, old boy?"

The amber light of the candle pulsed outward, throwing shadows in all directions, but neither sign or sound of Bright greeted them.

Alexander followed him in, and pushed the door shut behind them. It made the interior darker, of course, but something made him want the door shut anyway. It wasn't exactly as though he felt he was being watched, but all the same, he wanted to prevent anyone who wanted to from doing so.

Cleveland lit another candle, and handed it to him, mounted in an empty wine bottle. "I searched up the back last time, and couldn't find anything. I'll search up this end and around the fireplace, now. As I say, if Bright is anywhere, he's probably asleep over there. Why don't you go look behind the bar and see what you can find."

Alexander nodded, the candle doing very little to light his way. Yet, for all the darkness and mystery surrounding them, it was still the total silence that seemed the strangest. There ought to have been wind making the shutters rattle, or the door bang gently, or even just to whip eerily around the building, like something from a Gothic novel. The silence was somehow worse. The only sounds were their own footsteps as they explored the dark interior of *L'Agneau Abattu.*

Cleveland studied some books on a shelf above the fireplace. The only title he recognised was *Dracula*, all the others had French titles, a language of which he knew very little. He picked it up and flicked through it, and was a little disappointed - if not surprised - to discover that the text inside was all in French. He'd always wanted to read it, and he'd heard the American film version was very entertaining, although he supposed it wasn't the sort of thing that respectable gentlemen like himself should be seen attending. In any event, right now the last thing that he wanted to be thinking about was ghosts and horror stories.

"I don't think Bright came back here," he spoke gently, above a whisper, but still quieter than normal. "I'm worried he's bumbling around in that fog, still. If it affected him like it seemed to affect us and Father Geiger, then he could be anywhere by now. He could be at the tank, or Geiger's chapel."

"What do you make of him?" Alexander asked.

"Geiger? I think he's stressed out and confused. Whatever actually happened here, it was obviously very upsetting for him, and he's spent days - perhaps weeks, even - in a village all by himself. I dare say that something like that would get to the best of us. I suppose we're fortunate he's as lucid as he is."

"There's something about his story that doesn't add up."

Cleveland picked up something he had spotted on the floor. Standing up, he saw it was a packet of German cigarettes that had been crushed underfoot. Unwrapping it a little, he saw that three remained in the packet, and two appeared bent but undamaged. He straightened one out and lit it from the candlestick. He wasn't sure what he was expecting Nazi tobacco to taste like, but it turned out to be no different from any he had smoked at home; perhaps a little lighter if anything.

He saw Alexander was looking at him. "Sorry, did you want one?"

"No. I was saying that there's something about Geiger's story that doesn't seem to add up."

"I do know what you mean, and I think that's all part and parcel of his being confused. He's connecting dots that aren't meant to be connected. Jumping to conclusions, you know. His little fantasy world makes perfect sense to him, but I'm pretty sure there's a normal explanation for the fog, the disappearances, everything. As normal as you get in this part of the war, anyway."

The area behind the bar proved to contain very little of interest. A few broken bottles, some discarded cigarette ends, and a couple of dropped coins.

He let out a little yelp as his foot caught on an iron ring, attached to a trap door in the floor, presumably leading down to a cellar for storing wine, ale and anything else that needed to be stowed away. "There's a trap door here."

Cleveland straightened up and looked at him, his face looking otherworldly in the candlelight. "I doubt that Bright's hiding down there, but it probably bears investigating. There might be something down there that we can make a use of; even if it is only a bottle of wine or two."

He squeezed behind the bar, which was not the widest of spaces, and looked down at the hatch with him. "Doesn't appear to be bolted."

Alexander squatted down and took the ring in his hand and tugged. The door was heavier than expected and he had to change his position and grip to use both hands.

"Steady on, old bean, don't bust a gut," whispered Cleveland.

Alexander hunkered down, and straightened back up, lifting with his thigh and calf muscles.

The trap door opened and a ghastly stench billowed up and over them both. Cleveland swore colourfully, covering his nose and mouth with his forearm. Alexander had been hit by the brunt of it and felt dizzy. He spun sideways and vomited over the bar.

"Are you all right, there, Alexander?" asked Cleveland, his words muffled by his sleeve.

Alexander wiped his face on a nearby bar towel and nodded. "Yes, I'm fine. Ugh. God. What is that smell?"

Cleveland stepped back to the trap door and tried to peer down, but the candlelight didn't reach that far. "There's something down there, but I can't quite make it out. Maybe that was where all the food supplies were, and it's gone off?"

Alexander shook his head. "We've got to check it out. It might be important."

"God, it's rancid. What stinks like that? See if you can find a torch, or something. I know there's one in the tank, you know. I can't believe that I didn't think to bring it with us..."

Alexander looked up and down with the candle, exclaiming in success as he found a battered and rusted looking torch. He hit the switch, but no light was emitted. He shook it briefly and slapped it sharply against the bar twice, the percussive raps seeming jarring in the dark and still inn. The bulb inside glowed faintly, duller even than the candle light; then, after a few seconds, it spasmed into life and a strong, yellow beam shot out. It was bright - or, at least, it seemed so in the darkness of *L'Agneau Abattu* - though the beam itself was narrow, and did not illumine much outside of its path.

He stepped over to Cleveland at the side of the trapdoor, and gagged once more at the foulness of the air rising from within. Clutching a hand to his nose and mouth, he handed the torch to Cleveland.

Cleveland, stony faced, swung the beam downwards. "Oh, Jesus Christ."

The torchlight shone full beam on a waxy, pale, decomposing face. A woman, he supposed, going on the hair, matted and thick with blood. The eyes were sunken, the tongue bloated out of the mouth, and covered in small black bugs. He scanned the beam slowly, and saw an old man - eyes mercifully closed, this time - maggots feasting on his scalp and around the forehead where a bullet hole stood out, darkly. "Oh, fuck."

Each movement of the torch brought a new horror. Children, riddled with machine gun fire and thrown into the basement of the bar to rot. Women, eyes wide in terror, their clothes black and stiff with dried blood. A baby still in its mother's arms, half its head missing, replaced with a swarm of grotesque black flies, hovering around. Able farm-hands, old men, even a dog, shot and thrown into the basement of *L'Agneau Abattu.*

Alexander had thrown up again, and wiped his mouth with the back of his hand. "How many are there?"

Then Cleveland saw the booted foot sticking up from behind an old woman's armpit, an arm wedged between two bodies, reaching and clawing as if for assistance that would never come. "I...don't know. They're everywhere, and...god, it must be two or three bodies deep at least."

"It's the village. It's the whole bloody village!"

CHAPTER TWELVE

Alexander tugged at Cleveland's sleeve, trying to pull him away from the trapdoor. "Cleveland, we've got to get back to Franklin and report this. This is...this is bloody horrible! The Germans killed them all!"

Cleveland took one or two shaky steps back, and slammed the trapdoor back closed again. "The Germans are dead already, or a million miles away from here by now, but...Alexander, there had to have been at least a hundred down there, maybe two. Men, women and children butchered. Not even buried."

Alexander tugged at his sleeve again, his heart aching for the villagers and - strangely - also for Cleveland, who seemed so affected by their discovery. "We can report this back. Maybe there'll be an investigation, and they can find out who caused all of...this. There'll be a court martial, or something. Trust me, someone will pay for this."

Cleveland shook his head. "No. They won't. It'll all just get caught up and swept away in all the other horrors. God, Alexander. Those people. Mown down and thrown there to rot in the stinking basement of a pub. What the hell kind of ending is that?"

"It's a nightmare, Cleveland. A genuine nightmare. Look, we should get out of here, right? We've got to report all this to Franklin and O'Brien, at least. Let them know that Bright's not here, as well."

Cleveland fumbled a cigarette to his lips and lit it from the candle he had left on the bar. “Those fucking Nazis, Alexander.”

“Look, we’ll tell Franklin, yeah? It’s his command. He’ll know what to do. It won’t be anything that we have to worry about, okay?”

“We should level the whole fucking pub with the cannon. Let that be their tomb.”

“Sure. Right. Yeah. If Franklin says that we do that, then that’s what we do, yeah?”

They stepped backwards out of the pub into the village square, and pulled the door to the inn closed, the latch echoing inside.

It was only then that they saw the dagger embedded in its thick timbers. The steel was easily a foot long, and its hilt marked with a symbol immediately familiar to all participating in the war. Cleveland shivered. “That...that wasn’t there when we went inside, was it?”

It was barely a question, but Alexander shook his head, anyway. “No. No way. That’s an...an Ehrendolch, they call them. The SS carry them. That...there’s no way that was there. Cleveland, someone stuck that in the door while we were inside.”

“You think the Germans are here, after all?”

Alexander shook his head. “No, no I don’t. No SS officer would be parted from one of those. Yet, someone knew we were in here and...Cleveland, we need to get out of here. Something very strange is happening and I want to get out.”

Cleveland looked at his friend and nodded. “All right, lad. I’m with you on that score. Let’s just get back to the tank and we can...”

He turned slowly around, and fell silent.

The fog was everywhere now. All that could be seen of the village square was the cobblestones stretching about ten feet away from them, before being swallowed by the whitish-grey wall of nothingness. Alexander swallowed, the wet clicking loud in his ears. "The tank should be straight in front of us. We didn't make any turns on the way here. I mean, not the first time, that was what you said, right? It should be dead ahead."

Cleveland looked shaken, something perilously close to snapping inside his head. He yelled out into the fog "Franklin! O'Brien!"

Alexander snatched at his arm. "Keep your goddamned voice down! What if who ever put that dagger there is trying to follow us?"

Cleveland snatched the dagger from the door and pointed it threateningly at the fog all around them. "Who the bloody hell is doing this, huh? What's your bloody game?"

The hairs on Alexander's arms rose inside his shirt at the sound of a woman's voice, singing low, the contralto drifting across the cobbled street, the fog making its location difficult to pinpoint exactly.

"It sounds like Marlene Dietrich," whispered Alexander. "Is someone playing a record? What the bloody hell is going on here?"

Cleveland suddenly snapped his pistol up, and called out a challenge. "Who goes there? Show yourself!"

Alexander cast his eyes in the direction Cleveland was pointing his gun in and felt a strange chill at the sight of the shadowy forms of two - no, three - people gradually approaching them out of the fog. "Franklin? Is that you? Bright? O'Brien?"

Movement in the corner of his eye, and he drew his own pistol, turning and raising it in one smooth movement. "Hold! Who goes there?"

It was the shape of a woman - or so he assumed. He thought he could see the vague outline of a dress and a shawl move slightly as she stepped towards him, although he could make out no colour or physical details. Two children seemed to peek out from behind her legs, and then it seemed that suddenly more people grew into sight just behind her.

"Oh, fuck...Cleveland...Cleveland!"

Cleveland was squinting through the fog, confused as to why he was still unable to make out any of the shadowy figure's features. "Halt, or I fire."

"Cleveland, don't fire, man...I don't know what they want, but...fuck, Cleveland...we've got to get out of here, and we've got to go now!"

Suddenly, there were fifty or sixty shadowy figures around them, and it wasn't hard to imagine that there were even more in the background, gradually growing sharper and sharper, like a developing photograph. Alexander grabbed Cleveland's sleeve hard and shook it. "We've got to run for the tank. Run for the tank, Cleveland."

Cleveland did not seem to have heard him. "Halt, or I fire."

The three figures that had first approached them must only be ten feet away now, and Alexander began to imagine that he could see flashes of clothing, or even the vague impression of faces; though when he tried to actually focus on a detail it was as elusive as the memory of a dream, snatched away from his conscious mind. "Cleveland, run!"

He yanked hard on the man's sleeve again, then turned and ran off to his left, parallel to *L'Agneau Abattu*, the only gap in the advancing line of ghostly figures that he could make out.

Something in the desperation of his cry had obviously gotten through to Cleveland, as he finally snapped from his terror, cast an eye at the advancing crowd all around him, and bolted after Alexander, the voice of Marlene Dietrich still following them.

The sound of their boots stamping across the cobbled floor seemed deadened by the damp air around them, though Alexander now knew there was something simply otherworldly at work in the village of Demetier.

"Alexander," Cleveland called behind him, between panting breaths. "Where the bloody hell are we going?"

"I don't know," he yelled back, as best as he could manage. "Just away from that...that...from them!"

"Who the bloody hell were they?"

Alexander skittered to a stop as the fountain from the centre of the square suddenly rose into view. He didn't manage it as well as he would have liked and barked his knee on the concrete rim. "It's the villagers, Cleveland! The villagers of Demetier!"

Cleveland stopped just short behind him and panted for breath. "That...that's madness. The villagers are dead, Alexander. You just saw them. They're rotting in that fucking pub!"

"Yes. They're dead. Don't you see? The fog? The Germans getting ripped to shreds, like Father Geiger said? The villagers are the fog. They're haunting the whole fucking village!"

Cleveland shook his head. "No. That's goddamned madness, Alexander."

"Then what did we just see? You explain that to me, please!"

Cleveland sputtered and stammered for a moment, then rubbed his face with the palms of his hands. "Oh, god, Alexander, we've got to get out of here. I don't care if it's chemical weapons or ghosts or the 7th Panzer Division, this is just a really bad place for us to be."

"The tank can't be too far."

"All right. You ready to go again?"

"Yes, I think I-Jesus Christ!"

There, floating in the scummy water of the fountain, was the pig's head from the butcher's shop window. A German infantry helmet had been jammed tightly onto its swollen, rotting head, and a swastika carved between its eyes.

Cleveland paled. "An acquaintance of yours?"

"O'Brien found it in the butcher's shop, but it...it's been messed with, by someone."

There was a sudden coughing sound from behind him, and Alexander leapt to his feet, pulled his gun up, and saw Cleveland, eyes bulging wide, and the Nazi Ehrendolch from the inn door jabbed between his ribs. His hands came up to it feebly, and his eyes fell on Alexander, pleading for help, mercy and assistance.

Alexander froze and could only watch as a crowd of hands - old men's, young women's, leather-hard workmen's, dirty labourer's - reached from the fog and took a hold around his shoulders, his waist. An old woman's clawed, bejewelled fingers knocked off his helmet and sunk into his hair; though worst of all were the hands of children and babies that locked around his knees and ankles.

Cleveland held Alexander's gaze for a second - no more - and his terror was palpable. Then, as fast as they had appeared, the hands suddenly pulled back into the fog, dragging the poor man off with them, and Alexander once again found himself alone in the nightmarish fog.

He froze for a moment, shivering by the edge of the fountain, the horrendous Nazified pig's head bobbing gently in the fetid water behind him. He was just about to call out for Cleveland when he heard a voice gently sounding through the fog.

For a moment he feared that it must be the ghosts of Demetier returning once more, half-expecting it to be the disembodied voice of Marlene Dietrich calling him through the darkness, but then he began to hear odd words and phrases being exchanged, and in English this time.

"O'Brien, the Father here is getting twitchy as all hell. How's that engine looking?"

Alexander's spirits, previously flung down into the depths of terror and despair, were suddenly catapulted into a state of pure elation. He edged his way around the fountain and there, barely visible through the thick curtain of fog, was the Comet. He could just about make out Franklin standing atop the hull, shouting down into the darkness within, where presumably O'Brien was still labouring over the recalcitrant engine.

Letting out a little giggle of pure glee, he staggered purposefully towards them. He holstered his pistol and called out a greeting. "Franklin! O'Brien!"

He saw Franklin raise his hand to his brow and squint through the fog in his direction. "Alexander, old boy, is that you?"

The tank was growing rapidly into focus now, gaining colour and clarity with every step. "Franklin!" He called out again, when suddenly his adrenaline was completely gone, and he sank to his knees.

He didn't know how long he blacked out for, but the next thing he knew he was sat on the ground, propped up against the tank, with Franklin and Father Geiger squatted either side of him. The priest looked up at the tank commander. "He is alive, at least."

Alexander looked over at him, too. "Franklin, it's the fog, Franklin. The villagers of Demetier, they were killed, massacred. It must have been the Germans, Franklin. Now they've come back, and they won't let anyone leave the village alive!"

"Steady on, lad," Franklin spoke gently. "Where's Cleveland? Did you find Bright? The inn?"

"I told you. We found the inn, and all the dead villagers, too. They were just shot to pieces and thrown down into the cellar to rot. Their souls aren't resting, Franklin, they just aren't. They came back and they took all the Germans. They came back and they killed the Yanks that we were supposed to rescue. Now, they've killed Bright and they've killed Cleveland, and pretty soon they're going to come for us, too. I'll bet that's why the bloody tank won't work."

His energy spent, he kicked futilely at the ground and burst into sobs. "We've got to get out of here, Franklin. I saw them take Cleveland and, my God, man, the goddamn fear in his eyes! I don't want them to get me, Franklin, I just don't."

The priest looked at Cleveland. "I told you, didn't I? The fog itself is the root of all this evil!"

Franklin's face remained incredulous. "All right, father. Say I extend you the courtesy of going along with all this madness. What do you suggest we do? I'm down two men, now, and young Alexander here is all shell shocked. The tank won't turn over, and..."

He was cut off by the sound of Marlene Dietrich's *Lili Marlene* drifting across the square. The atmosphere suddenly changed, growing thicker, and tinged with a physical sensation like static electricity. It was as though a church bell had been struck, but a bell so vast that it was felt rather than heard. Franklin got to his feet and looked out into the fog. "There's someone there. Bright? Cleveland? Is that you?"

Alexander clambered to his feet, pulling himself up by the tank's bogeys. "It's them, Franklin. It's them. The villagers. We've got to go, now. This is how they got Cleveland, skip. This is how they got Cleveland!"

Father Geiger grabbed hold of Franklin's arm. "We have to go now. Run. We run back to the church. I don't know why but they've never managed to get in there. Maybe it's the holy ground? This whole village is plagued by devils and it may be the only safe soil in the area. We have to go there now!"

Franklin took a shaky step backwards as he began to discern more shadowy figures approaching through the fog. "Yes, I...I think you might be right, Father. Which way is the church from here?"

"It should only be a hundred yards or so, but I told you before how this place messes with your sense of direction."

Franklin popped the fastener on his sidearm holster and stepped back from the advancing shadows quickly. He balled up a fist and banged on the hull of the Comet. "O'Brien, abandon tank!"

"What?"

"Abandon tank!"

There was a dull thudding and clanging and O'Brien's red face emerged from the turret. "What's happening, Franklin? Alexander, what's up with you? Where's Cleveland?"

"I'll explain on the way, O'Brien. Go. Now. Follow us."

O'Brien was too smart a soldier to question a direct order, and abandoned his tools, firearm and helmet, and hurriedly slid down the cold, damp hull of the tank. As soon as his boots hit the cobblestones, Father Geiger gestured them to follow him and ran off into the fog.

Alexander, still shaken, was the last to get moving and found himself bringing up the rear. He was just running past the front of the tank when a woman's arm shot out of his blind spot, her fingers instantly clawing at his face and hair. He screamed. Her touch was ice, and her nails cut like razor blades. He felt another hand grab at his jacket sleeve, and he hurriedly wriggled out of it, shucking it to the floor. He ducked low out of the woman's grasp and pelted across the cobblestones, chasing the barely visible form of O'Brien moving through the fog.

CHAPTER THIRTEEN

It seemed as though they were running for hours, through an endless sea of grey, before the church suddenly appeared before them. Father Geiger let out a cry of joy and relief at the sight of it, bolting up the path, leaving the kissing gate in the wall swinging behind him. By the time Alexander reached the main doorway into the church, Franklin and O'Brien were already in the main room, and Father Geiger pushed the door shut behind them, throwing a massive bolt into the wall with a satisfying thud.

All seemed quiet, then, though their every movement was amplified a hundred fold by the size of the church hall. Father Geiger stopped Alexander with a hand on his upper arm. "You are bleeding, my friend."

Alexander raised his hand to his face, and winced. When he brought it away, his fingertips were red with blood. "Franklin," he called into the church. "I think I'm hit. I'm bleeding."

Father Geiger led him to a pew, and Franklin and O'Brien hurried over to assist. The commander took some cotton and bandages from his side pouch and dabbed the blood away. "You're not hit, old bean. Just looks like something scratched you up. Did you run through some brambles, or fall into some barbed wire, or something?"

Alexander's heart leapt into his mouth. "No, nothing like that. There was a woman out there. She lunged at me and - dash it, Franklin - I thought that was it for me, then. That was how they got Cleveland, you see? Just these cold, dead hands coming out of nowhere, and then - whoosh - he was gone. I thought they had me, but I threw off my jacket and managed to pull away. Is it bad?"

He winced as Franklin dabbed off a little more. O'Brien broke the silence. "It'll not be fatal, if that's what you're worried about, but, well, you'll have a few good scars for your trouble, I dare say. Nothing awful, mind. Hell, it might actually suit you!"

Father Geiger smiled, trying to lighten the mood as well. "Yes, it could make you look rather dashing, I think. Mrs. Alexander will be happy, I'm sure."

Alexander had to chuckle at that himself. "Is there a bathroom or a water closet I can use, Father? I want to wash up, and see for myself."

"Of course, my son. Through the door there is my office, and there is a toilet just on the other side. Please, be my guest."

Alexander nodded his thanks, and could already feel a fresh dribble of blood running down the bridge of his nose.

Franklin turned to the priest. "All right, I believe you. There is something inhuman here, and it is not going to let us escape easily. Now, you said earlier that the fog came for the Germans, and then a few days later, it came back for the rest of the village. What I don't understand is who all those...oh, dash it...who all those ghosts in the fog were. There must have been a hundred of them if there were twenty."

Father Geiger shrugged. "I don't know. It doesn't make any sense. None of this does."

O'Brien lit a cigarette and then hesitated for a moment, expecting a rebuke from Father Geiger which never arrived. "Well, what are we going to do? Our best hope of getting out of here was the Comet, and we've just run away from it. We're stuck here in this church just the same as Father Geiger was before we arrived."

Franklin cocked an eyebrow at the priest. "Is there another way out of here? An old sally port, or something?"

Geiger shook his head. "If there is, then I don't know where it would be. No-one mentioned anything when I took up residence here."

"We're stuck," spat O'Brien. "The only place we're safe is this here church, and there's no way to get a message to the outside world from here, I suppose? No, of course not. I dare say someone will come looking for us, but that may not be for a week, or maybe more; if the front moves while we're here then it could be weeks before anyone wonders what became of us. We could just be written off as 'lost in action' inside of a month, you know. Besides all of that, if anyone does come looking for us, they're going to wind up stuck in this stinking fog just the same as we are. I'm plumb out of ideas, Lieutenant."

Franklin leapt to his feet, and smacked his fist on a pew out of frustration. "No, dash it all, just no. I won't accept that this is how it ends for us. There has to be a way to solve this riddle."

Father Geiger shrugged. "Is there some way we could disperse the fog?"

"You said sunlight has no effect, heat does nothing, it would seem. In any event, it's patently obvious that this is no ordinary fog, Father. No, this fog is...you know, in every ghost story I ever heard, the reason that the ghost walked was because it wanted something. All those M.R. James and Edgar Allan Poe stories I loved when I was at school were full of shades and spectres trying to complete some mission or quest that wasn't able to be completed when they were alive. If this fog is a supernatural manifestation - and I think there's no doubting that by this point - then it must be after something. Tell me again why you think the fog came?"

Geiger shrugged and went to the lectern. Reaching down, he pulled up a bottle of wine, presumably liberated from *L'Agneau Abattu*. "I told you. It came for the Germans, after they killed those people. Two men and a woman were killed. The Germans moved into *L'Agneau Abattu*, and then the following night - or maybe the next - the fog came for them."

He walked slowly back to them, yanking the cork from the bottle. He took a swig and handed it to Franklin, who accepted it gratefully, before taking a slug of his own. "That doesn't make any sense. If the fog wanted to avenge the deaths of those villagers, then why would it come back and kill all of the rest of them the following night?"

***

Alexander switched on the electric light in the small bathroom and studied his face in the mirror. The claw marks that the spectral woman had left were not deep, but they were long, and were still weeping a little. Three jagged lines ran from the centre of his forehead to just shy of his right ear, and another marked from below the middle of his nose across most of his right cheek, descending down and fading along his jawline. He supposed he could tell people it was a shrapnel, or a barbed wire injury.

He needed some sort of story. No-one, not even his parents, would ever believe the truth.

He grabbed a towel, ran it under cold water for a second, then tried to clean up the wounds a little. If they were going to end up running through the fog again sometime soon - as he suspected that they might - then he didn't want to do it with eyes full of his own blood.

He discarded the towel, now stained a pale pink, onto the floor. The scratches had welled up again. Perhaps there was a first aid kid somewhere in here that might be able to help.

Spotting a wooden cupboard in the corner of the room with the key still in the lock, he decided to try his luck and clicked it open. Some ministerial clothes - cassocks and vestments and so on - hung from a pole running its width. Looking down, he spotted some mothballs, and a wooden crate that seemed overflowing with clothes, topped by a leather coat.

Thinking it odd that the priest of Demetier would be a keen motorcyclist, he plucked at the jacket, and discovered that it was much larger than his initial impression had suggested. It was, in fact, a great coat, at least five foot long from shoulders to hem. Double breasted, with a silver belt buckle at the centre.

He felt his arm hair starting to rise, and his heart fell into his stomach. Cold adrenaline and tingling nausea flooded his bloodstream.

There, pinned to the upper arm, was the crimson skirted Swastika, the flag under which the German forces had been operating since 1920.

***

"I told you. It came for the Germans, after they killed those people. Two men and a woman were killed. The Germans moved into *L'Agneau Abattu*, and then the following night - or maybe the next - the fog came for them."

He walked slowly back to them, yanking the cork from the bottle. He took a swig and handed it to Franklin, who accepted it gratefully, before taking a slug of his own. "That doesn't make any sense. If the fog wanted to avenge the deaths of those villagers, then why would it come back and kill all of the rest of them the following night?"

The door to Geiger's office burst violently open with a crash, and Alexander stormed out, pistol raised and aimed at them. His face was crimson with fury.

Striding forward boldly, he kept the pistol trained on the priest and positively spat out, "Because he's a fucking liar!"

Geiger straightened instantly, yet did not raise his hands in surrender. Instead, he bravely faced down his accuser, as Franklin and O'Brien got to their feet around him. O'Brien reached bravely out and tried to grab at Alexander as he stormed past. "Easy, lad, easy! What's all this about?"

"The fog never killed any of the villagers. His story doesn't make sense, does it? He's twisted it to suit his own little alibi."

Franklin stepped forward, holding out a palm in a 'stop' gesture, hoping to ease the private into relaxing a little bit. "All right, Alexander. We're all tense. We're all worried here. Why don't you tell me what you think you found out."

Alexander kept the pistol trained on Father Geiger, and fumbled with his left hand into his pocket before pulling out a small card and throwing it to the commander. "He's not a priest. He never was. His name's not even Geiger."

Franklin picked up the card and studied the photo. "Officer Johann Seeliger," he read aloud, finally glancing up at O'Brien and the priest. "Schutzstaffel. Himmler's finest."

The man they had known as Father Geiger gave nothing away. Alexander kept the pistol trained on him. "I found a full uniform out back, minus the cap. Greatcoat with those little lightning bolts and everything. He's a fucking Nazi, sir."

Bright popped his holster open and smoothly drew his own weapon. "We found an SS cap in the inn, Cleveland and I. Your man here must have been running scared of something to leave his precious little hat behind."

Franklin raised an eyebrow at the man in priest's clothing. "This is your photo. Do you deny that you are Johann Seeliger of the SS?"

Seeliger hesitated, then shook his head. "There seems to be no denying it, now. Yes, I am Seeliger."

"All right. You are to consider yourself captured and a prisoner of war. Do I make myself clear, Herr Seeliger?"

The SS officer stole a quick glance at the two pistols trained on him and licked his lips nervously. "Given the circumstances, I accept. This does nothing to change our present situation, however. We are all prisoners at present. If we cannot get out of this accursed village, then there is no point you aiming weapons at me and calling this a victory."

O'Brien lowered his revolver. "He's got a point, Franklin. We need to figure out what this fog wants."

Alexander shook his head, his face a mask of pure anger. "Not until I get some answers, first. Okay, Seeliger, why don't you tell us all what actually happened?"

Seeliger shrugged and sat on a pew, seemingly unconcerned by the gun still pointed at his head. "We were told that there was a resistance cell operating near to the village of Demetier. Some of the villagers were running food and supplies to the group, which was camped out somewhere in the surrounding farmland. They were also sending and receiving messages on their behalf. We could not pin down the freedom fighters themselves, so we were told to cut off their means of supply.

"By this time, as you know, the German army was already retreating. Our Führer overplayed his hand to the East, and should have listened to Rommel when he had the chance. Instead we are exhausted against Russia and overrun by you fine gentlemen and the Americans."

"Yes, our hearts bleed," sneered Alexander. "What happened to the village?"

"I took command of a squad of infantry. We did what we needed to do."

"Say it."

Seeliger took a deep breath, and looked the young man in the eyes. "There were three that we suspected of being spies above all the others. Two men, and a young woman. We executed them in the village square. Unfortunately, the young woman's...perhaps it was her son, or perhaps her younger brother...he ran in to try and save her at exactly the wrong moment. It saddens me to say that he was caught in the crossfire."

Alexander brought the butt of his revolver down onto the bridge of Seeliger's nose. There was a stomach churning crack, and the German flinched, emitting a strangled grunt. His nose hung strangely and bright red blood ran down his mouth. Alexander pointed the gun back at his temple again. "Don't say 'crossfire'. You gunned down unarmed men, women...and children...that's not a goddamned crossfire, you Kraut piece of shit."

Seeliger spat out a dribble of blood and glowered at Alexander. "The boy ran out and was cut down. The village revolted at this and - for my part - I understand their outrage. Their assault was impotent, however. They were unarmed, and we had assault rifles and machine guns. Things got out of hand, very quickly.

"We tried to cover up as best as we could, and hid the bodies in the basement of the inn. I didn't want them to remain food for crows, but we lacked the time or the ability to make a proper grave. We stayed in the village for one night, or at least part of one night. It was then that the fog came down, and my men were lost."

Franklin reached out and took the gun from Alexander. "That's enough, lad. All right, Seeliger. How did you escape?"

"I don't know. I just ran through the fog and made my way here. I hid, I scavenged supplies...all else is as I already told you, I swear it."

CHAPTER FOURTEEN

"We throw him outside," spat Alexander. "We throw him outside, that's what we do. Don't you see? That's why the fog is still here, why the undead aren't able to move on? They're trapped here, because they can't finish taking revenge on the fucking Nazis who put them in the ground. Hell, he didn't even put them in the fucking ground, did he? He threw them into the cellar of a pub to fucking rot!"

Franklin kept one eye on Seeliger, and held out a palm to Alexander. "Easy, lad. Let's try and be rational, here. We don't know what's going on with that goddamned fog. If we throw him out there, then who knows what will happen. Maybe they'll go into a feeding frenzy and tear the whole goddamn church apart. You ever think of that?"

"The fog doesn't know what it wants," put in Seeliger. "Your American friends found that out, not to mention your two crew mates. If the fog wanted me, then why would it attack anyone else, huh? That doesn't make any sense."

Alexander shook his head and jabbed a finger at Seeliger. "You don't get a say in this. Those Americans and our crew mates are dead because of you; because of this land that you cursed. That's why. They can't rest, because you murdered them in cold blood and didn't even give them a goddamn decent burial. Now Cleveland and Bright and all the others have been dragged off to who knows what level of hell, because of your act of pure evil."

Seeliger smirked, and held out his hands, palms facing toward Alexander. "I was only following orders. You think your army would have acted any differently had they needed to plug an information leak?"

"That...no. We would never, that's just...you Germans are just animals!"

Seeliger smirked again, jerked his arm, and a Mauser pistol dropped into his hand from his cassock.

Franklin yelled and went to shove Alexander out of the way.

Seeliger smoothly raised the gun and fired, the muzzle flash striking out like a magic blade.

Alexander let out a cry as a burst of crimson spurted from Franklin's side, and the tank commander fell down onto the hard church floor.

The German SS officer, still in his priest's disguise, went to fire again at Alexander, when O'Brien's fist shot out of nowhere and snapped his head sideways. Seeliger staggered into one of the pews, shifting it a little, the screeching groan of wood on stone echoing through the church. Instantly he tried to right himself, but O'Brien was already upon him, striking him twice more in the face.

Seeliger spat out blood, one of his front teeth missing now, and tried to push the Mauser around to get a close quarters shot on O'Brien. Alexander glanced at Franklin, laying on the floor, his hand pressed desperately to his wounded side, then back to the struggling figure of O'Brien. The SS officer was twisting and turning the gun, straining to get the barrel lined up with O'Brien's chest. The Comet driver had spotted this, however, and gripped the man's wrist with all his might, trying to thrust his hand against the pew to force him to drop his weapon.

Alexander hurriedly squatted next to Franklin. "Franklin, are you all right? Is it bad?"

Franklin hissed in pain through clenched teeth and rolled onto his injured side, pressing down on it as hard as he could. "It hurts like a bugger. Don't know how bad it is. Help O'Brien. Stop that Kraut."

Alexander, still squatting on the ground, turned on the spot, and sprang forward, throwing himself at the grappling soldiers. He caught Seeliger side-on in a first-class rugby tackle, throwing him sideways onto the floor, and pulling O'Brien along with him, causing them to fall on the floor in a tumble of arms and legs. Seeliger's boot pulled back and struck forward, kicking him hard in the face, and he felt the gouges across his forehead open up again.

O'Brien was the first to his feet, pulling a revolver of his own from his holster, and pointing it directly at the prone German. "Arms up, lad. Drop the gun."

Seeliger's eyes were nothing short of pure hatred. He seethed anger and pent-up violence from every pore. Nevertheless, he held up the Mauser loosely in one hand, and let it clatter to the stone floor with an echo. "I know when I am beaten, Englander. Very well."

Alexander clambered to his feet and - confident that O'Brien had the SS officer covered with his revolver, ran back to the injured Franklin. The commander had wriggled himself into a sitting position, propping his back up against a pew, his hands clutched tightly to his side, though the dark red stain was spreading worryingly fast. He cracked a smile at Alexander, though his face was growing pale. "I knew I could trust you two to handle it."

Seeliger, still on the ground, kicked hard at O'Brien's ankles, then swept his legs round in a circle. The older man lost his balance and fell down hard, his revolver skittering down the aisle. Seeliger spotted his chance straight away, grabbed his Mauser in a two handed grip, jumped to his feet and began backing away from them. "Stay down, English! You will not take me!"

O'Brien shook his head in a daze, and raised his hands. "You lot never stop playing dirty, do you? If it's not firing torpedoes at merchant ships, it's kicking Jews out of their homes."

Seeliger sneered, backing toward the altar, and the main door. "Silence! I've had enough of your eternal groaning and grumbling all the time. The sun has not yet set on the Third Reich. Heil Hitler!"

O'Brien raised two fingers, the back of his hand facing the German. "Hail Churchill."

Alexander grabbed Franklin's revolver from his hip holster, turned in a crouching position, aimed, and squeezed off a round in the direction of Seeliger. His aim was wide, however, and the top of a pew's backrest exploded in a shower of splinters and dust. This still caught the Nazi officer by surprise. He let out a startled grunt, and threw up his arm involuntarily to protect himself from the debris. Alexander squinted one eye closed and tried to draw a bead on him from his awkward position on the floor, but wasn't able to before the German rallied and fired off two rounds from his own pistol. One echoed off into the darkness of the church behind him, but the other struck the floor worryingly close to where he and Franklin lay.

O'Brien grabbed his own revolver from where it had fallen in their brief scuffle and crouched behind one of the thick oak pews. He fired off three bullets in rapid succession but none found their mark.

"There's no point trying to escape, Seeliger," Alexander shouted in the sudden silence. "There's nothing outside but the fog - the undead you helped create - and all they want is for you to step outside so that they can tear you apart!"

"I'll not end the war as a prisoner," Seeliger yelled. The vast room and high ceilings made his voice echo and reverberate, but Alexander assumed he must be hiding behind either the lectern or the main altar.

"You already are, lad," shouted O'Brien. "You've been trapped here since the day you killed those people, don't you see that? You're the first one to fall victim to its curse!"

The Mauser sounded again and O'Brien threw himself to the floor as the seat of the pew he was hiding behind sprouted a large hole.

"I think I have an idea," Alexander shouted.

"What?" O'Brien shouted over to him.

"Just trust me, all right?"

Franklin gripped his arm. "What are you doing? I've lost too many men already."

"Just trust me, and be ready to run as soon as you can."

Alexander shifted into a position as closely resembling a runner on the starting blocks as he was able. Then, with a final nod at Franklin and O'Brien, he got up and ran perpendicular to the altar, heading full speed to the side wall, dominated by a huge stained-glass window, depicting Jesus and the resurrection of Lazarus. As he ran, he sang at the top of his voice, the exertion giving it a strained, falsetto quality.

"Göring has only got one ball, Hitler's are oh so very small! Himmler has something similar, but Goebbels has no balls at all!"

His jingoistic taunting drew the attention he hoped for and he felt a bullet strike a pillar behind him, and another whizz a mere inch above his head. Fearing that at any moment he would be struck down by one straight to the head, he was positively elated as he skidded to a stop by the stained-glass window, and threw himself to the ground.

Seeliger leapt to his feet in the sudden stillness, extended his arm out towards Alexander and fired three rounds from his Mauser.

The bullets all shot over the prone form of Alexander, and hit the stained-glass window behind him. The penetrated glass seemed to hang in the air for a second, before cascading to the floor with a deafening noise that was part roar, part clatter.

The waterfall of glass fell to the floor, revealing the churchyard beyond.

After a second or two's hesitation, the fog began rolling and creeping through the broken window. Thin, grey tendrils eased and slipped over the broken lead strips, danced over the remaining red and green splinters, and seeped up and over onto the floor.

Alexander got to his feet in an instant and ran back towards O'Brien and Franklin. "Run! Into the back room!"

O'Brien didn't need telling twice, his adrenaline from the gunfight spurred on by the hairs on the back of his neck rising at the distant chorus of *Lili Marlene* carried on the wind. He reached Franklin at the same time that Alexander did, and the two of them lifted him up, dragging him towards the sanctuary of the back room as fast as they could.

Seeliger's Mauser pistol barked twice, but they did not stop to return fire.

Alexander stole a quick glance towards the shattered window and could see the shadowy figures within the fog stepping forward into the church. The woman striding forward purposefully, the child jumping and skipping with glee, the men marching solemnly. Even though he could make out no physical details, he could sense the story and the life that each of them carried with them.

Looking back at the altar, he saw Seeliger discard his spent pistol, the colour draining from his face. If he turned and ran, there was every chance that he'd catch up with them, but fear had paralysed him. He was a man who saw his fate before him, and knew that this time there was no escaping it.

Franklin's toecaps scraped across the floor as they dragged him the last few feet. "Hurry. They want Seeliger, but who knows what will happen if they chance to see us here as well."

The fog was positively billowing into the church hall now, clouding their way to the office doorway. It had been plainly in front of them just a second ago, but now it was suddenly as though they were back in the village square, by the Comet and the fountain. Alexander let out a sob of relief as he physically collided with the wall, his shoulder just scraping the doorframe.

O'Brien fumbled with the door handle and they threw themselves inside. Before so much as the merest tendril of fog could make its way into the back room, Alexander kicked the door shut behind them, and pressed his weight against it.

For a moment there was silence.

Then came the sound of the panicked footsteps of Seeliger running back down the aisle towards them. The sound grew closer, then farther away again, off to the side. "My friends," he shouted. "Please, I beg of you! Help me!"

A strangled cry of anguish came from far away, and Alexander shook his head slowly. "They're toying with him. He's run back up to the altar again. Remember how it seemed to mess with your sense of direction? The fog is giving him the run around."

"Like a cat with a mouse," whispered O'Brien.

The German called for help again, the voice growing louder. "Please! You can't leave me out here! They'll kill me! Please, friends!"

None of them looked at each other. Franklin was sat on the floor, back against the wall, pale and exhausted. O'Brien leaned against the desk, heaving his revolver back into his holster. Alexander stood, his weight against the door.

The sudden pounding at the door caused them all to flinch, but none moved to answer it. If anything, Alexander leaned harder against it.

"Please, I beg you! I'll confess my crimes in court! I'll become a model citizen! I'll join up and fight alongside you! Just open the verdammt door! Bitte! Please!"

Lili Marlene grew louder, stronger. The pounding sped up. “Oh, god, don’t leave me here to die like this! I’ll do anything you want! Anything!”

Alexander caught Franklin’s gaze. The commanding officer’s face was blank, and conveyed no emotion or command. There was simple, indifference there. Alexander grimaced, frowning and pulling his lips inwards. Franklin nodded slowly, understanding. There was nothing to be done. Nothing that should be done. This was simply the world correcting itself.

The pounding grew quieter, the voice falling into a whimper. “Goddamn, you. If you don’t open this door, you’re no better than I am. You hear that? You’re just as bad as I am.”

None of them looked at each other after that.

The pounding faded, the singing grew. Alexander plugged his fingers in his ears, but they could not stop the piercing final scream when it came.

Lili Marlene faded instantly.

They sat there, each lost in their own thoughts.

Alexander eventually broke the silence “Should we...?”

Franklin looked at his watch. “It’s...my watch has stopped. What time is it?”

O’Brien checked his. “It’s eight thirty. PM, that is.”

Franklin nodded drowsily. “Let’s just...rest here. I think what trouble there is is gone, but if it isn’t, then I’d rather wait until dawn to face it. Set an alarm for...”

His head fell sideways. Alexander got to his feet nervously. “Is...is he?”

A loud, obnoxious snore emanated from the commander, and the relief that he felt was palpable.

“You know what the real crime is here?” O’Brien asked. “He has the bloody temerity to claim that I’m the one who snores in that bloody tank.”

CHAPTER FIFTEEN

Alexander awoke gently, his back aching from where he had slept propped up against the door. Franklin was awake already. Although still rather dozy, he had regained a lot of his colour from the previous night, which Alexander took to be a good sign. The gunshot wound would require medical attention as soon as was possible of course, but it at least appeared that the commander was not quite at death's door. A strange whistling noise drew his attention to the far side of the room, and he saw that O'Brien had a kettle boiling on a small stove, and a strong, earthy smell drifted toward him. "What is that?" he asked. "You've got to be joking me! I haven't smelt that in a year."

"Oh, yes, lad." O'Brien smiled at him. "It's real coffee. None of that acorn and thistle piss that we've had to put up with. Looks like either Seeliger - or the real priest of the village - had a decent stash of proper coffee put aside. There's no milk, so you'll have to take it black, but, well, I think that that just adds to the flavour, don't you?"

He passed a mug to Franklin, then another to Alexander. He inhaled the aroma deeply and couldn't stop himself from smiling. It was the first good thing to happen since they had left the base. "How are you feeling, Franklin?"

"Well, the bleeding's stopped, so I'm hoping that's a good sign. It's bloody painful, though, if you'll pardon my language.

Still, I'll get seen by the doc back at base, and they'll have me right as rain in no time."

"We need to get out there and take a look at the tank," muttered O'Brien. "Oh, don't worry. I intend to sit here and drink this coffee just as much as you do, but we need to be back on the road, soon."

"We'll head straight back to base," reflected Franklin. "We're down two men, Alexander and I are injured...to be honest, O'Brien, you've come out of this rather lightly, haven't you?"

"Sir, I'm insulted by that. I'm the one who's going to be bending over at all angles and in all weathers fixing that tank so we can get home. I can assure you that I'll be suffering the most out of all of us."

Alexander stood, straightening his back. "In all weathers, you say? What do you suppose that the weather is like outside?"

They fell silent, and drank their coffee.

***

Alexander turned the door handle, and pushed gently. What he saw outside made him turn his head in disgust. "Oh, god. Oh, fuck."

Officer Seeliger lay sprawled out on the floor, his head thrown back. His SS Ehrendolch had been forced upwards into his throat and the tip of the twelve-inch blade lay somewhere inside his skull. The resulting pool of blood stretched far around the corpse, and as much as it repulsed them, they had to tread through it to leave the back room. They looked at the body for a while, could think of nothing to say, and so turned away.

"Would you look at that," said O'Brien, the hint of a smile curling his lips, as he pointed towards the wall where the window had been shattered and fallen to the ground in a rainbow of shards.

Alexander was a little behind him, supporting the still injured Franklin, and it took him a little moment to take in what O'Brien was showing him. Beyond the now empty window frame lay the town square of Demetier. The fountain still at its centre, and across the way he could see the butcher's shop, the inn where the villagers lay, and all the other shops and houses. The Comet sat not too far from the fountain, its main hatch still open, where they had abandoned it the previous night.

"The...the fog's gone," smiled Franklin. "Would you look at that? It's clear as a summer's day out there!"

Alexander nodded. "Yes, it's over. I guess the villagers finally found peace; or some sense of justice at least."

O'Brien lit a cigarette. "It's really a rather pretty little place, isn't it? I hate that a thing like...what happened...happened here. Well, I don't like that it happened anywhere but, well, you know what I'm getting at don't you?"

Franklin nodded. "I know what you mean. There's been precious little good to come out of this whole stupid affair; but I believe that a lot worse would be happening if we - and plenty of others like us, of course - weren't here to stop Mister Hitler and his evil agenda. Germany's time is running out - has been since Normandy - but there's a way to go yet, I fear."

Alexander kicked a few shards out of the way, and the three of them stepped through the window frame and into the churchyard. The sun felt good on their skin - it seemed as though it had been positively days since they had last felt its warmth.

"What do we do next?" O'Brien asked.

Franklin sighed. "We go back to the base, I suppose - if the tank will turn over, right enough."

"You don't want to go looking for Bright and Cleveland?"

"No, I...I don't believe they can be found. I just hope that wherever they are they can find the same sort of resolution to all this that the villagers did. Some sort of satisfaction, if nothing else."

"What do we tell top brass? They had families back home who'll want answers."

Franklin looked weary again. The brief celebration of their victory over Seeliger and The Fog had lifted his spirits, but - as he had said - there was a way to go yet. "I don't know. We tell the truth as much as we can, I suppose. We ran into one surviving SS officer and...they were killed. Reclaiming the bodies wasn't possible. That will have to do I think. It's not perfect but, well, it will have to do."

The fountain was still, but the water was clear. Alexander still had no desire to touch it, fearing that the pig's head may still be sunken in it somewhere.

They reached the tank and - for O'Brien, at least - it felt as though they were home already.

Alexander pushed the shell into position, slammed the cover and secured it.

"Ten degrees left," Franklin shouted down into the tank.

"Ten degrees left," Alexander relayed to O'Brien, who was filling in the gunner's seat.

With a whining groan, the turret rotated slowly to the left.

"Target in sight," O'Brien yelled. "Ready to fire!"

Alexander leaned over to shout up to Franklin. "Ready to fire!"

"Fire," Franklin replied.

"Fire!"

The whole Comet rocked on its tracks as the main seventy-seven millimetre cannon fired, sending the seventeen-pound shell speeding across the village square. The warhead collided with the stone walls of *L'Agneau Abattu*, belching dust and smoke outwards. The wall shuddered and slowly began to fold in on itself.

The crew eagerly repeated the process and a second shell joined it several feet to the left, punching a square through the oaken door and detonating inside. Fire and black smoke shot out and upwards, as the inn collapsed, the fire spreading through the wooden furniture and roof.

Franklin climbed out and onto the hull of the Comet, and O'Brien and Alexander soon joined him. The remains of the villagers of Demetier were now buried under the rubble. It was not what they deserved, but it was better than they had received at the hands of the Nazis, and at least they were there now to stand witness to their ersatz funeral.

"Does anyone want to say a few words?" asked Alexander, but he received no reply.

They stood and watched the fire and the smoke for almost half an hour before Franklin grew tired. "We need to be making a move. There's no good us waiting here any longer."

"Aye," agreed O'Brien. "Maybe the fires will spread, take the whole damn village with it. That'd be sort of nice, in a way, don't you think? If there was nothing left and it all just turned back to countryside again? It might almost make up for the damage the war did here."

Franklin clapped a hand on his shoulder. "I know what you mean, old friend. I know what you mean."

The engine of the Comet turned over successfully, and its six-hundred horsepower roar filled their hearts with courage. The tracks moved, guided by Franklin and driven by O'Brien, and the tank turned almost on the spot, before pushing back the way it had come and toward their home base.

Alexander was riding on the hull - partly because they were hopeful that there would be nothing for a loader/operator to do on the short ride home, but also because he wanted to keep an eye on the still injured Franklin. The bullet was still lodged in the man's side, somewhere, and he would need constant supervision.

"What do you suppose Seeliger meant?" he asked, watching the landscape crawl by them. A plane flew high overhead, too high to make out what it was, but he assumed that it must be an Allied supply drop of some kind.

"What do you mean?" Franklin asked, lighting a cigarette.

"Back in the church, there, before he kicked off. He made some sort of crack about how our side would not have acted any differently. Do you think there's any truth in that?"

Franklin thought for a moment, then exhaled a cloud of smoke, gazing off at the horizon. "Do I think that our side would have massacred an entire village, purely on the suspicion that one or more of them were passing information to the enemy? No, I don't. I don't think that that's the way we do things. Of course, that's not to say that we - as a nation - won't have done some bloody terrible things by the time all this is said and done."

"How do you mean?"

Franklin shrugged. "War's not easy, and for a lot of people - military or civilian - they'll have to do some things they can't quite believe they're doing in order to survive. If your family was genuinely starving, would you steal food from someone in your village? Would you kill them to get at it? These are fine theoretical questions for us, right here, but for someone out there, possibly only a few hundred miles away, they're very real."

"What Seeliger and his troops did wasn't a matter of survival."

"No, I suppose not. If you're asking me about the real darkness and evil out there...well, yes, I think that doesn't take sides."

"What do you mean?"

Franklin tapped the ash from his cigarette and watched the ember. "You've heard all the stories of how the Jews are suffering in Germany and Poland, yes? If it's true - and I personally see no reason to believe that it isn't - then there's absolutely nothing there that is inherently a German thing. It's not tied to the German people, or the land or anything like that. I would be so bold as to say that there's more than a few people at home that would agree with what's happening there. People in parliament, people in your street, teachers at your old school, probably even people in your extended family. They'd all be more than happy to ship their neighbours off to a labour camp, given half the chance."

"That's not exactly a very comforting thought."

"Evil is not a comforting though, Alexander. Not ever."

CHECK OUT OTHER GREAT HORROR NOVELS

BLACK FRIDAY
by Michael Hodges

Jared the kleptomaniac, Chike the unemployed IT guy, Patricia the shopaholic, and Jeff the meth dealer are trapped inside a Chicago supermall on Black Friday. Bridgefield Mall empties during a fire alarm, and most of the shoppers drive off into a strange mist surrounding the mall parking lot. They never return. Chike and his group try calling friends and family, but their smart phones won't work, not even Twitter. As the mist creeps closer, the mall lights flicker and surge. Bulbs shatter and spray glass into the air. Unsettling noises are heard from within the mist, as the meth dealer becomes unhinged and hunts the group within the mall. Cornered by the mist, and hunted from within, Chike and the survivors must fight for their lives while solving the mystery of what happened to Bridgefield Mall. Sometimes, a good sale just isn't worth it.

GRIMWEAVE
by Tim Curran

In the deepest, darkest jungles of Indochina, an ancient evil is waiting in a forgotten, primeval valley. It is patient, monstrous, and bloodthirsty. Perfectly adapted to its hot, steaming environment, it strikes silent and stealthy, it chosen prey: human. Now Michael Spiers, a Marine sniper, the only survivor of a previous encounter with the beast, is going after it again. Against his better judgement, he is made part of a Marine Force Recon team that will hunt it down and destroy it.

The hunters are about to become the hunted.

CHECK OUT OTHER GREAT HORROR NOVELS

DEATH CRAWLERS by Gerry Griffiths

Worldwide, there are thought to be 8,000 species of centipede, of which, only 3,000 have been scientifically recorded. The venom of Scolopendra gigantea—the largest of the arthropod genus found in the Amazon rainforest—is so potent that it is fatal to small animals and toxic to humans. But when a cargo plane departs the Amazon region and crashes inside a national park in the United States, much larger and deadlier creatures escape the wreckage to roam wild, reproducing at an astounding rate. Entomologist, Frank Travis solicits small town sheriff Wanda Rafferty's help and together they investigate the crash site. But as a rash of gruesome deaths befalls the townsfolk of Prospect, Frank and Wanda will soon discover how vicious and cunning these new breed of predators can be. Meanwhile, Jake and Nora Carver, and another backpacking couple, are venturing up into the mountainous terrain of the park. If only they knew their fun-filled weekend is about to become a living nightmare.

THE PULLER by Michael Hodges

Matt Kearns has two choices: fight or hide. The creature in the orchard took the rest. Three days ago, he arrived at his favorite place in the world, a remote shack in Michigan's Upper Peninsula. The plan was to mourn his father's death and figure out his life. Now he's fighting for it. An invisible creature has him trapped. Every time Matt tries to flee, he's dragged backwards by an unseen force. Alone and with no hope of rescue, Matt must escape the Puller's reach. But how do you free yourself from something you cannot see?

Printed in Great Britain
by Amazon